REVENGEFUL PUNKS

DOLLS AND DOUCHEBAGS PART FOUR

MADELINE FAY

To freaking Eddie Munson.
Leader of Hellfire Club.
Rock on lost soul.
Sincerely,
Obsessed fan of Stranger Things Season Four

BLURB

Have you ever had the breath knocked out of you? A gasping breath stuck in your throat, tightness growing so thick that you think this might be it? I'm going to lay down and maybe never get back up.

Blending into the darkness, wanting to disappear because the one thing that scares you the most comes knocking right at your door.

I've come this far and survived, but how much more can I take?

With Logan, Nicky, Tey, Dalton, and Dom at my side, can I find the strength to stand up again and fight back?

The men surrounding me aren't good guys. They hurt without remorse, but I'm coming to realize, I don't want the good guy who comes riding on a white horse to rescue me.

I want my villains to corrupt my soul until I'm standing on top with my hands drowning in blood and jewels dripping from my fingertips.

Gone is the innocent, scared girl who ran and ran. In her place is a woman taking control of her life.

Tillie is no more. My life ended the moment I met my psycho guys, and I was reborn with revenge in my veins.

I became very, very bad, and it feels really, really good.

TRIGGER WARNING

This is a dark, bully, enemies-to-lovers romance story ending with a cliffhanger. A why choose romance where the heroine won't have to choose between her different love interests.
This book contains graphic and violent scenes, including rape, physical and emotional violence, child abuse, swearing, sexual scenes, PTSD, and MM. Suitable only for readers aged 18+.
Chapter Fourteen contains light MM.
Spoiler: This series does NOT contain cheating.
Please do not take this warning lightly if you are sensitive to any of the triggers listed above.
This is Part Four of Dolls and Douchebags, which does end with a HEA eventually, you will just need to wait until the next book.
If you have any issues regarding this book, please reach out to the author using one of the links on the contact the author page.

PROLOGUE

Cruz

"I've never seen your face before, Cholo. My dealing goes through Payne only. You wear his prez patch, so I'm going to go out on a limb and guess you killed him?" Carlos gestures to my new patch, not taking his stare off me as he leans back on his beat-up couch and turns his attention to the whore in his lap, ignoring me now.

My gaze roams around the living room of the leader of the Los Muerte gang, taking in the dirty carpet with cigarette burns, the walls with holes the size of a fist, and the stolen products scattered across the floor. I expected nothing less, knowing he runs a small gang. He's trying to take the other gangs off the streets, but in order to do that, he needs to make friends in higher places. Everything this guy represents makes me grind my teeth. If you want others to respect you, then fucking make it to the top by yourself. Killing, maiming, beating the shit out of someone, that's how you instill fear and make sure no one stabs you in the back.

Worthless piece of trash.

Loud bass music from the speaker makes the floor vibrate, the overly obnoxious rap annoying me and loud laughter from his gang members littering around the house. I want respect, and Carlos is obviously throwing disrespect in my face, acting like I'm not the president of my charter, which starts to piss me off. He thinks I'm just some other club member, a fill-in for Payne until someone else comes along. I can see he thinks he's the bigger threat by the way his posture is relaxed into the couch cushions as he smokes a joint, his brown eyes flicking over my dirty biker boots, all the way up to my faded jeans, the vest with my new position on the patch, and my long, blond hair slicked back.

Fuck him.

I'll rip out his right eyeball and the teardrop tattoo he has under the left corner of his other eye. That will teach him thinking he can dismiss me as not a threat. I want his fear. He's nothing, just another rat that follows the rest of the colony, and that's why he'll die in this fucking trash hole of a house.

"No. That honor has to go to whoever sent his head in a box to my club. They didn't have a return shipping label, so I can't show my gratitude. It came to my attention that Payne was looking for something he lost, and you just happened to find it?" I appear nonchalant, making my body relax, even though I'd like nothing better than to murder every fucking gang member in here and carve my name into their skin.

Carlos takes his eyes off the whore sitting in his lap, his stare immediately settling on mine again to notice the quiet, intense way I'm watching his every little move. He's finally noticing there's a predator in his house. My eyes want to roll into the back of my head in pleasure as he stares at me warily, a hint of fear flashing in his eyes as he eyes his gun on the coffee table before he tries to mask his expression from me. No one can fool me, I've been wearing a mask half my life.

"Lost? What could he have lost? Why does it interest you so much? Perhaps a shiny diamond Payne misplaced?" Carlos tries a different angle to gain some power back, to taunt me, wanting to dangle Tillie in my face, just because he can.

"Oh. That shiny diamond was never too far from me, and I plan on getting it back one way or another. You catch my drift, amigo?" I calmly state, watching as his eyes roam over me, noticing I don't have a tattoo or anything resembling the club except for my vest.

"Hmm. I hear you." He nods his head and pushes the woman off his lap, her ass falling to the floor at his feet. "Leave us." She quickly gets to her feet, tugging her skimpy dress over her ass as she flees the room. The pounding bass of the music stops, his gang members leaving out the front door until it's just me and Carlos. "I'm going to be honest with you, *Cruz*. You aren't from my hood, and I don't fucking know you. Why should I help you?" He takes a hit off his joint before tilting his head, eyeing me through the haze of smoke from the weed puffing out of his mouth, blowing the stench in my direction.

"Ah. It's like that, is it? Let's cut to the chase. What do you want?" My fingers twitch at my sides, wanting to wrap around his thick neck that's covered in tattoos and squeeze the life out of him.

I cross my arms and lean on the wall closest to me with a relaxed posture even as a hundred different ways of killing him runs through my head. Maybe I should just get it over with and carve him up, but he has me intrigued about what he wants so badly.

All in due time, after I get what I want. It's all a game and I plan on being the winner on top.

"What every man wants... power. These are my streets. I

grew up in this very house. I take care of my neighborhood, and seeing a man just fucking waltz in, taking what's mine... I don't think so. Fucking cops." He smashes the blunt on the coffee table and rubs his hand over his shaved head in frustration.

So the cops are involved. Very interesting.

"I know the feeling. Payne never deserved to be president of my club. It seems we have that in common. You want the cops off your back?" I raise a blond eyebrow at him, having no problem slashing some throats in my spare time.

The more bodies I have to practice on, the more it helps get my initials perfect.

"It's more than the pigs. It's who's running the damn city when it's mine. The drugs coming in and going out onto the streets should be mine, while I count *my* money behind my desk." Carlos curses in Spanish, upturning the coffee table in front of him like a toddler throwing a tantrum.

I don't even flinch or move away from the wall as I watch him lose his mind instead of thinking clearly. This is why he's a bottom-feeder and will die that way, where no one cares as he rots away.

"You get me what I want and I'll get rid of those standing in your way." I smile, feeling the fake stretch of my lips as the lie slips through.

I'll have Tillie at my feet, hiding her away from the rest of the world until she only has eyes for me. Her king. Taking over these other gangs will only add to the power at my fingertips.

Carlos takes a deep breath, swiping his tongue over his gold tooth as he considers me before taking another joint from his jean pocket, straightening it out, and lighting up.

"I know exactly where she is, but it's not going to be easy to get to her. She's surrounded by all the guys she's fucking.

The whore," Carlos says, his meaning clear as he passes the joint to me.

My eyes burn, tears collecting at the corners as I inhale the weed between my lips. She's the only one who can cause me these emotions. I feel nothing while killing anyone but one thought of her being mine forever has me almost crying. My whole body shakes, wanting her to be right in front of me, to cut into her skin until everyone can see who she belongs to. Pent-up rage crawls up my throat, hanging by a thread, but I have to control the anger until the moment is right. She better start praying to her God now because if she's really letting other men touch her... I might just have to kill her and keep her corpse by my side forever. She'll never escape me then.

"Do we have a deal?" Carlos' dark eyes gleam like he just hit the jackpot. The fucker probably thinks he can stab me in the back once he gets what he wants.

I'll beat him to it.

I pass the joint back to him, blowing the smoke in his face. "You have the Demon Jokers at your disposal."

He takes the weed back with a slow, shit-eating grin. A silent agreement that we work together, for now... until one of us is dead.

It won't be me with blood spilling from my neck like a river.

I'm coming for you, Tillie.

Finally.

Tillie

My breath saws in and out rapidly, and each draw of oxygen into my lungs feels heavy. I can't breathe. The need to claw at my skin grows the longer I'm laying in the dark of the trunk. It's hot and sticky, making pieces of my hair slip from my ponytail and stick to my sweat-slicked cheeks.

"Peaches."

My eyes can't focus on anything, they keep shifting around, looking for any means of escape. I notice that my fingernails hurt and are wet, probably from clawing at the lid of the trunk like a wild animal.

Just fucking open!

Why won't it open? I want out. I need to get out before they deliver me into Cruz's clutches.

Oh God. I'm going to be sick.

"Tillie!" Violent tremors wrack my body, and my eyes snap over to the source gripping my upper arms. Blue. Bright, blue eyes. A gaze I always seem to drown in, happily sucking all the oxygen out of me until I'm desperate to breathe again. Tey. "That's it. Focus on me, peaches. Take a deep breath. Feel me, baby." Tey releases my arms from the tight grip he has on me and clasps my cold hands, placing them against his warm chest.

Thump.

Thump.

Thump.

His heartbeat is racing, but his gaze is direct and calming as he stares at me in the dark trunk. He's right here with me. I'm not alone. He holds me so close that his minty breath washes over my face, the tip of his nose against mine.

"T–Tey," I stutter, my lips trembling as I try not to get lost again in a panic attack.

My nails dig into his skin, almost wanting to claw my way into his heart and stay there. Blood coats his chest, either mine or his, maybe both.

"I know you're scared right now, but I need you," he whispers, slamming his palm on the ceiling as the car swerves around a corner too hard, knocking us into the opposite metal frame.

Maybe we'll die before we even make it to our slow death, our necks snapped from the reckless drivers as we're thrown around back here.

"We're going to die," I state the obvious, my panting breath fanning his face as he peers down at me before going back to inspecting the taillights.

Those things aren't going to pop out, even if he tries. Besides, what's he going to do? Stick his hand out of the hole and hope someone sees? People these days pretend to not see shit because they don't want to get involved. Can't say I blame them.

"We aren't going to die. At least not here. I kind of pictured us dying together with something epic, like fireworks and shit. Maybe a sinking boat? But you better share the fucking door with me, or we go down together. Stupid, fucking Rose," he mutters under his breath, reaching up to wipe a tear from the corner of his eye before he starts kicking at the taillight behind him.

"Are you crying?" I ask, sounding ludicrous to my own ears, wondering if maybe I'm actually dreaming and I'm back in bed with the guys surrounding me.

"Naw. I'm allergic to assholes I couldn't kill," he replies in a serious tone, his white teeth shining in the dark as he glances down at me with a smirk.

"Didn't know you were allergic to Logan this whole time," I drawl out sarcastically, unable to help myself, even as I'm panting through each suffocating breath while tightening my arms around him.

"There she is. Do you think we can bang out a quickie before we arrive wherever we're going? Wonder if I can pump you full with more of my cum? Practice makes perfect. I'll add your period to my calendar so I know when we can start to make babies," Tey coos softly, dropping a quick peck on my parted lips as I stare up at him like he's insane.

Well, he is crazy, but still.

"We'll talk about this later when we aren't about to die, okay? I'm not ready for babies," I say in shock while grasping his bicep as the car swerves again before it starts to slow down.

"Whatever you say, baby mama. I totally get Dom now, and I'm glad the man is on board." Tey shuffles in the tight space, giving the taillights one more kick with a muttered curse under his breath. "Okay, game plan. Kill everyone, then get back to fucking. I just need you to play dead for now."

I feel like my mind is spiraling and I'm kind of relieved it's Tey stuck here with me because everything that comes out of his mouth is crazy and distracting but gets my attention through all the panic. He slides my panties out of my hair that I used as a hair tie earlier and quickly slips them up my legs, back into place covering my pussy. He moves me around so easily, like a ragdoll, and any other time, I'd find it extremely hot how he can just throw me around any way he wants.

"How do you expect me to play dead, and what the hell are you going to be doing?" I shake my head to clear it, letting my limbs relax as he arranges my body just as the car completely stops and the engine cuts off.

"Playing dead right here with you. It catches people unaware and makes them think you're weak. Don't do anything until I do, okay, lover? Just keep your eyes closed and steady each breath you take," he explains, crossing my arms over my chest like I'm actually dead before I end up smacking his hands away and relaxing them at my side.

"Fuck," I whisper hoarsely as I hear the car door open and slam shut, boots crunching on gravel.

"I'm right here," Tey promises before letting his head slump to the side and closing his eyes.

He does look like he's dead with all the blood coating his face after being ganged up on and beaten. He acts like he doesn't even feel the pain and I'm beginning to realize there is more to Tey than I know. I'm determined to keep getting to know him, and that thought alone has my body relaxing while my eyes close just as the trunk opens.

"Fucking pussies. Don't know why Carlos said to be careful with the blond one. A few hits and he's out cold." One of the men standing over us scoffs and slides his hands under my body to pick me up.

I make sure my body is limp, hopefully making his job harder with my body being deadweight. I hate the feeling of his hands on my skin, especially when he squeezes my ass cheek before tossing me over his shoulder like a sack of potatoes. The only thing keeping me from screaming my head off is imagining hacking this fucker's hand off and shoving his middle finger up his ass, and, of course, Tey being here. I have to believe he won't let anything happen to me. He'll kill everyone, let his psycho flag fly free if anything hurts me.

"Jesus. This bastard is heavy. Carlos, grab his feet." Someone swears, grunting as they grab Tey out of the trunk.

I peek through my hair as we start walking inside some building, my arms swaying limply with each step of my captive's stride. Two guys are carrying Tey behind me; one grabbing his feet while the other has his wrists. I know Tey is getting a kick out of them grunting, sweating, and shuffling their feet as they carry his ass around.

I try to count how many times we turn a corner and whether we go left or right, but not being able to see clearly makes it feel like we're walking through a maze. For some reason, it smells like tacos and smoked meat. I think we're in a restaurant.

Finally, at some point, he stops and swings open a door. The sound of heavy clunking and a buzz fills my ears the moment we step into a room, and the hot blast of a heat wave fans my face.

"Dump him right there, and make sure those chains are tight," the guy holding me commands before he bends and drops me onto the cold, concrete ground.

I'm instantly sweating from the heat of the room and having déjà vu of being in a basement. The guy does something above me, and I hear the sound of metal hitting metal before I feel the cold steel placed around one of my wrists.

Fuck.

They laugh above our prone bodies, making it difficult to keep my breathing even as one of them talks about the vile things he wants to do to me. I'm only wearing my skirt and bra, but luckily these fuckers are scared little shits about blood.

"Shut the hell up. This bitch bled all over my fucking shirt," the one who carried me says in disgust.

Who's the pussy now?

It's just a little blood and completely fucking normal.

"Filthy cunt," I hear one of them spit out, followed by the shuffling of feet until their voices sound further away and a door bangs closed. I wait, count to ten, and slowly open my eyes.

The first thing my eyes connect with is Tey's bright blue ones right beside me, holding my gaze before a small smile forms on his lips. He's making sure I'm okay and looks relieved that I'm not spiraling into a panic. At least, not at the moment.

"I'm okay. Where are we?" I glance away from him, taking in our prison cell as sweat rolls down my spine.

Copper pipes hang from the ceiling, which is what's making the clicking noise as the steam generator pumps out heat, and the danger signs plastered to the walls makes my stomach queasy. We're in a boiler room. No wonder it feels like my skin is melting off.

"We're in a Mexican restaurant," Tey says, standing up slowly before arching his back as best as he can, and letting out a groan.

I climb to my feet too, grimacing at the soreness between my legs and the sticky feeling of Tey's cum coating my thighs. At least I'm not bleeding too bad, though I never do on the first day. Small miracles.

"How do you know?" I ask, puzzled as to how he knows where we are.

"Saw the sign as they were carrying us in. Angel?" Tey's tone comes out so serious and deep that I have to turn back to him. I've never heard him without a hint of a smile in his voice. "I need you to take off your skirt and rip a piece off to tie your hair up away from your face. I'm going to strip too."

My brows scrunch, confused as he uses one hand to start tugging off his pants until he's kicking off his shoes and socks at the same time. He stands back up and arches a brow when he notices I'm not doing as he said and I'm just staring at him like he's lost his mind.

"Tey... we aren't having sex right now," I tell him very slowly, as if it's a foreign language to him.

"Baby, my sweet cherry, the woman of my desires, I'm glad your mind goes straight to the gutter with me around, but the clothes need to go. It's fucking hot in here and I don't need you passing out on me. Strip." He winks and turns his attention to the shackle around his wrist, tugging on it to test its strength.

I watch him, realizing we aren't going anywhere as he grunts, his muscles tensing with each pull on the metal that's connected to a thick pipe bolted to the floor. My gaze slides down his back, watching the delicious muscles shift as his shoulder blades bunch together. The tapered, perfect V of his hips has my mouth watering, and the moment my eyes get to his incredibly muscular ass, a laugh bursts out of my mouth before I can stop it.

His underwear is a light, blush pink with two whole peaches on each butt cheek, and the writing just below his waistband says *sweet cheeks.*

"Find something funny, peaches?" He turns towards me

and I get a view of the front of his underwear, where there's more writing right over his dick.

Juicy.

I drop to my knees, tears clouding my vision as I clench my stomach in pain from laughing so hard.

"T–Tey. Oh, God. Please don't ever change. I freaking love you," I breathe out through my laughter, glancing up to see him staring down at me with so much hunger in his gaze that I immediately sober up.

"You can't say stuff like that to me and not expect me to fuck your juicy pussy," he mutters darkly, his voice rough as he reaches around me and unzips my skirt until it pools around my ankles.

"Get us the hell out of here, Tey, and you'll have access any time you want." I gesture towards the space between my thighs, feeling the low, pulsing throb of how empty I feel and the butterflies in my stomach from just the thought of him pushing his big cock inside me again.

"I'll hold you to that promise, but knowing the guys, you're going to have to be wide open with a red light because my guess is they're already looking for us. Be prepared for your pussy to know the shape of all of our cocks and to be walking like a cowboy for the rest of your days." He wiggles his eyebrows at me before sitting down so he's leaning against the pipe we're chained to while grabbing my skirt.

I step out of the way and shuffle closer to him, plopping down on my ass right next to him with a heavy sigh. I don't care that it's hotter than hell in here and I'm melting like a popsicle, I need skin-to-skin contact with him to ground me. He rips my skirt into strips and holds up a piece in my face.

"Turn," he demands, and I comply, giving him my back

with my head bent near his chained-up hand so it's easier for him to put my hair up into a ponytail.

His fingers slide through my messy hair, untangling knots and causing me to tilt my head back towards him more. I'm not used to being taken care of or the gentle way he handles me. He's tough enough to send people running the moment they make eye contact with his wild, blue gaze, but once Tey decides you're someone important to him, he'll move heaven and hell to protect you. I know without a doubt I'm one of those people, and I'm glad I get to see this side of him. Although, I love his psycho ass too.

"Where did you learn to do this?" I ask, my voice coming out drowsy and content.

He's quiet for a little bit, finishing up tying my hair into a high ponytail before I sit up and turn back towards him. He slides some flyaway strands behind my ear and sighs as he drops his arms, closing his eyes with his head tilting towards the ceiling.

"You know I grew up in foster care, bounced from house to house. It made me the way I am today. Every person who beat me down, the ones who told me I was a nobody and always would be... I don't want that for the other kids. It's the reason I stay where I'm at even though I'm eighteen. Someone has to look out for those kids, tell them they can make it out of here one day and be somebody. So, yeah. You need pigtails, a messy bun, or braids, I'm your guy. You'd be surprised how bossy an eight-year-old can be when she wants her hair a certain way, and people say I'm crazy... Girls are scary." He pretends to shudder and glances at me out of the corner of his eye, his cheeks turning red.

Oh. My. God.

My ovaries are doing strange things, tightening and

making it difficult to breathe, because right now, I want to give this man all the babies he wants.

I'm losing my mind, but that was the sweetest thing I've ever heard, and now it's my life mission to see him, or any of the guys, holding a tiny baby.

"I'm too freaking young, Tey, but damn, if I don't want to have a gazillion bab—" My mouth snaps shut when the doorknob rattles and someone starts to walk in.

My heart pounds, the blood draining away from my face as a boot appears first, then a dirty jean pant leg, leading up to a vest that's so familiar it makes me sick to my stomach, and finally, into eyes that give me endless nightmares.

"Hello, little bird. My, my. You escape your cage and make all sorts of *interesting* friends, but don't worry, I'm here now to bring you back right where you belong. Did you miss me?" Cruz's voice comes out emotionless, but the dangerous glint in his eyes causes my vision to blur as if I'm going to pass out any minute.

I just might. I'd rather be having my nightmare of being back in that fucking basement at the compound than actually having him stand here right in front of me. I'll slit my wrists first before ever ending up in his clutches again. I want to say something, anything to show I'm not afraid, but my throat closes as my chest heaves up and down in panic.

"Hey, fuck face. Get fucked, you dirty cum stain!" Tey shouts, drawing Cruz's attention away from me to flick a fleeting, annoyed glance at Tey before he gazes back at me.

Cruz doesn't see Tey as a threat. He wouldn't, thinking he's above everyone else. I don't want him even looking or thinking about Tey. His attention needs to stay on me, no matter what, because he'll punish me if he knows I have feelings for anyone else.

"I didn't miss you. Honestly, I forgot you existed," I reply back smoothly, trying to make my voice sturdy, but I think my trembling bottom lip gives away how terrified I am.

"You forgot me? Forgot how I pounded into your virgin asshole, making you sore and bloody? You can't forget me, Tillie. I'm engraved in your skin. You hold scars I put there, and the scar tissue around your puckered asshole will always be a reminder that I've been inside you. Cover your body in tattoos to hide our time together, but make no mistake... I own you." My world tilts on its axis, narrowing down until I can see only his eyes as he hurts me over and over again. My screams echo in my head from that night, making me wonder if I really did escape or if I've been dreaming of freedom this whole time. Something that will never be within my reach. "Now you're getting it." Cruz crouches in front of me and slaps me hard across the cheek with no warning.

My head whips to the side from the force of the blow as I blink tears away. A whooshing sound is pounding in my ears, but I can see Tey yelling when my gaze clashes with his furious one. The burning on my cheek pulses, but this isn't the first time I've been hit. Years of Payne taking his anger out on me and his obedience lessons have made it easy to push past the pain.

"I'm going to kill you," Tey whispers so quietly and deadly that it causes goose bumps to break out on my arms.

Cruz ignores him, stroking the back of his hand over my stinging cheek before reaching for my hair like a cobra striking its prey. He tugs me closer as I yelp at the sudden hard grip.

"Time for obedience lessons." Cruz's menacing eyes contain the only emotion he'll ever show. It shows just how sick he really is.

I am nothing. I feel nothing.

Time is running out for me, but I refuse to show my fear in front of this sociopath. Even if I'm gurgling on my own blood with my last breath, he won't have the satisfaction of knowing the fear that consumes me in his presence.

I'll die before giving him another piece of me.

"Fuck you!" I scream in his face with everything inside me.

CHAPTER 2

Nicky

Jin: Remember your place, Son, and don't disappoint me. Be at the dock's warehouse in two days at eight o'clock sharp. Bring the girl.

I've read and reread the text from Jin over a dozen times. Doesn't matter that I've already seen it, my fingers are gripping my phone so tightly that I'm surprised I haven't cracked the screen. I've put up with a lot of his shit through the years, always bowing my head and obeying, like any good son would do.

No more.

Part of it has to do with Tillie. She's opened my eyes, like I've been sleepwalking my whole life. For someone so tiny and fragile-looking, she's one of the bravest motherfuckers I know. We all have our stories... and the shit we've been through. There's just something about her facing all her fears, after being knocked down so many times, that makes me want to keep getting up each day to see her take down everyone in her path.

I want to do better, be someone that she and Tey can look at, and know I will never run. I'll be right here, through thick and thin. Even Logan and Dalton need to feel secure, that when a moment comes and they have to leave their backs exposed, they need to know I've got them. Fuck it. Dom too. How he stares at Tillie tells me he's in it for the long haul. Sometimes you just know from the first glance that one person is going to change your fucking life.

So having Jin tell me to bring Tillie to the auction, like she's only good for one thing because she's a woman, makes me want to murder him, gouge his eyes out for even staring in her direction, and have his tongue ripped out for telling me who's good for me. You can't help what the heart wants, and the small organ in my chest wants to devour Tey and Tillie, locking them up tight so they'll never leave me.

I realize I'm staring off into space, not paying attention to whatever lecture our calculus teacher is droning on about when my phone pings with a notification. The teacher keeps talking, pretending she doesn't see me with my cell out and not listening to a word she says. She knows better than to try anything with me. All the staff knows who my family is and no one wants the triad coming after them. It's usually done at night, involving a death you never see coming, like sleeping peacefully in your own bed until you wake up gasping for air as a knife slides along your throat, ending your miserable life.

I huff a sigh and pray for my own sanity that it's not Jin messaging me again. Leaning my elbows on the desk, I bring my cell up to my face and arch a brow when I see a video in the group text.

What is Tey up to? Doesn't he have a class with Tillie right now? Turning down the volume, I push play and almost fall out of my seat. I'm not sure if I blink or even breathe, all my focus is on the screen as the video starts playing. The first thing I notice is Tillie in the front seat of my car in only her bra and skirt. Her head is tilted as she stares at Tey, confusion in her brown eyes right before a small smirk graces her plump lips. That smile is naughty, devilish, and sinful. I watch, as if transfixed, unable to look away as she swings her leg over to the other seat and braces herself over my stick shift. My pants become tight, my cock straining against the zipper as she slowly lowers herself, her pussy lips stretching over the gearshift as she fucks herself on it.

I'm going to kill Tey for this. Are there panties in her hair? It's obvious they fucked and he's torturing me. He was supposed to wait for me so we could fuck her together. Is he pissed at me? They're both playing a very dangerous game, and their punishment will not be light for what I have in mind.

My chair squeaks against the floor as I suddenly stand up and walk out of the classroom without saying a word. By the time I'm in the hallway, the video has ended and bubbles are popping up as someone texts.

Dalton: Fuck me hard. I'm supposed to be heading to a church meeting but change of plans. Ever been fucked on a motorcycle, little bitch? You're about to.

Logan: You're dead, Tey. If anyone saw her like this, I'm burning their eye sockets out and having you dig your own grave. No one looks at what's ours.

Dom: GET TO THE PARKING LOT NOW!!

My heart starts racing at Dom's text. I expected him to tell Tillie how beautiful she looks, but instead, his message sounds frantic.

Down the hall, a door smashes outwards and my head snaps up to see Logan running towards the front of the school. I don't hesitate to follow after him as I run to catch up, but I slow down for a second as Paris and her two friends drag her down the hallway between them. One of the girls holds paper towels under a bloody nose as they disappear into the nurse's office. I shake my head to clear it as my thoughts run wild, the fast beating of my heart telling me just how Paris got the two black eyes with a busted-up nose. I slam through the double glass doors into the California sunshine, sure that Tillie knows why. It's a gut feeling, and if true, there's going to be hell to pay.

It's blistering hot as I sprint outside and around the corner towards the parking lot on the side of the school, passing a shit ton of fancy cars until I see my Nissan come into view. My breath saws in and out, taking in the scene with one glance. I feel like I'm about to explode out of my body in rage, destroying everything in my path. One of Dom's members is pacing back and forth, talking on his phone in rapid Spanish as Logan kneels down next to the dead gang member who is bleeding all over the parking lot. I bend down next to my car and pick up Tey's unicorn, carefully placing it in my pocket before surveying the inside of my car without touching anything.

I'm going to get the prints of every fucker who touched my car and bury them alive with only enough oxygen to make their death slow.

"Mother fucking asswipes!" Logan spits out in fury, kicking the gang member over and over, even though he's dead.

"Don't touch anything!" I bark at him, gesturing for him to take over looking for anything in the car that might help.

He kicks one more time and takes a deep breath while shoving his fingers through his hair so not one piece is out of place. A show of calm and collected, but he's anything but that.

"You!" Logan narrows his eyes and strides over to one of Dom's guys who's currently freaking out and keeps making a sign of the cross over his chest. "What the fuck happened?" Logan growls, grabbing the guy by his collar and snarling in his face.

I walk around my car and pop the trunk, moving the tarp and shovel out of the way until I find my extra laptop tucked away in a safe case. Never know when you might need it since I'm always breaking into shit and destroying lives from behind my computer screen.

"I was just watching the girl like Dom ordered since he couldn't be here, but then she started having s–sex. I didn't watch! I–I was tr–trying to keep myself busy as they were having fun in the car. By the time I saw them throwing the girl and guy in the trunk, I was too far away." Logan pushes the babbling gang member away in disgust and starts swearing in Italian, reaching for his gun as if he might just kill the guy right here and now.

"Logan, call Dalton. He's blowing up our phones, freaking the fuck out," I mutter, giving him something to do so he doesn't lose it and my phone won't stop vibrating in my pants pocket.

Unzipping my case, I pull my laptop out and get right to work. Hacking into the school campus security cameras takes only seconds, it's sometimes too easy. I need to hack into the Pentagon or something to make it a challenge, but that's for another day. I block out Logan growling and cursing into his phone and everything else around me as I pull up the video feed, saving it to my drive and wiping the original from the school computers.

Can't have them seeing the dead body or Logan who's about to murder one of Dom's guys. His father's reach can only go so far. The FBI is a different aspect that Franco hasn't dipped his hands in... yet. At this point, I don't think either of our fathers gives a shit about us and would let us take any downfall to save their own asses.

Leaning against the trunk of my car, I rewind the footage and feel my cock twitch in my pants as I zoom in on my car about thirty minutes ago. Tillie's riding Tey in my backseat like her life depends on him, rutting against him so hard that my back tires bounced in a hypnotic rhythm each time she slid down on Tey's cock. I didn't have to zoom in to see what they were up to. Honestly, I just want to watch.

Taking a deep breath, I fast-forward, groaning as I look at the time to see how long they were roughly fucking. I push play as Tillie climbs into my front seat, saying something to Tey as he lounges in the back. I already know what I'm going to see, but I can't look away. Tillie grins and gets into position over my stick shift, lowering herself with her head tossed back in pleasure.

I grind my teeth, loving the look of heat and desire crossing over her face.

"What the fuck is taking so long?!" Logan pants next to my ear like an angry bull before he turns my computer towards him to get a look at what has captivated me so much.

Guess I've been standing still without saying or moving for a while. My pulse races and my whole body locks up tight. I have a very sudden urge to tie Tillie and Tey up, hold them captive in the sweetest torture for fucking without me.

"What did Dom's guy say?" I clear my throat and yank my computer out of his grip, fast-forwarding before I get distracted again by Tillie's sweet pussy and Tey's big dick.

"Nothing. Fucker fell asleep on the job. Just woke up to them gone and a dead body left behind. I'll let Dom handle him." I glance away from the screen for a split second, seeing Logan's hands shaking.

I get it. I want them both back, and if anything happens to them... may God have mercy on the fucker's poor soul for touching what's ours.

There's a rumble of motorcycles as Dalton and some of his club members enter the school parking lot. We'll most likely have students glancing out the windows soon to see what's happening. Before that happens, we need to get the body out of here.

I watch as Dalton comes to a halt a few feet away and swings his leg off his bike, marching over to us with a murderous expression.

"I'm out of this fucking school for two days and you fuckers can't keep an eye on my little bitch. Where the hell is she?!" Dalton is shouting at this point and getting in Logan's face like it's all his fault.

Logan stands up straighter, his expression darkening as he steps closer to Dalton and shoves him back a step.

"Fuck you. Just, fuck you!"

Logan is losing it. His shirt is wrinkled, which has never had a crease in it since I've known him. He likes things clean and in order to have some control in his life, but that control he holds on to so tightly is slowly slipping from his grasp.

I pause the video and use my hands to pull them apart before they start swinging fists at each other.

"Knock it off. We don't have time for this shit show," I state in a calm voice, even though I'm anything but.

The sound of screeching tires pulls our attention towards a Dodge Challenger slamming into the middle of the parking lot, and as the door opens, Dom steps out. He leaves the door open and the engine running as he walks over to the guy who was supposed to be watching our girl. Without stopping or saying anything, Dom pulls out a gun with a silencer on it from the back of his pants and shoots the guy point-blank in the forehead.

"Son of a bitch. Axel, Lucky, carry the two bodies to Dom's trunk and get rid of the rest of the evidence. Not a drop of blood is to be left behind." Dalton barks out orders, running a hand down his face in irritation.

"Just play the fucking video," Logan rasps out, stepping towards the back of my car again with Dalton hot on his heels.

Breathing through my nose, I place the laptop on the surface of my trunk and wait for Dom to join the three of us. No point in replaying it again. It's just wasting time when we could already be on our way to rescuing Tillie and Tey.

"This video better have some answers or I'm going to go on a killing spree," Dom says, buttoning his suit jacket with his jaw clenched.

My fingers fly over the keyboard and I try to pull up audio as the video starts playing again, but these types of cameras don't come with the ability for us to listen in.

Fuck.

Still, we all watch as a shitty-ass car without a license plate pulls up next to mine in the video feed. Men in black masks jump out quickly and yank my backseat car door open. From both sides, they grab Tillie and Tey, ganging up on Tey as they obviously see him as a threat. Watching him being kicked and punched has my heart stopping and my breaths coming out ragged.

"He's still alive," Logan says softly next to me, reaching out and squeezing my shoulder in reassurance.

I don't say anything, just shake my head to focus on the video once more in case anything sticks out. We watch Tillie slit one of the fuckers necks, making me instantly proud of her before she's thrown into the trunk right along with Tey.

"That's our girl," Dalton whispers and rubs at his chest, like he's in physical pain watching them fight for their lives.

"We don't know jack shit. The dead fucker had a tattoo on his neck but it was blacked out with another tattoo. This has to be Carlos, but where the fuck do we start?" Logan mutters, pacing back and forth as he runs his hands through his hair in frustration until it's sticking up at all angles.

"I'm not so sure about that. Looks like we have a Peeping Tom." Dom points to the screen. Three cars down sits a very familiar person hunched in their seat.

All four of our heads jerk up at the same time and we look at the passenger seat through the windshield, watching Gary trying to sink down farther in his friend's car.

"The little weasel. I'm going to kill him this time." Logan grins, looking a little unhinged as he strides over to a panicking Gary as he fumbles, trying to lock the car door, but his butter fingers keep slipping.

I slam my computer closed and put my hands in my pockets as I calmly walk over, wanting to wring his little fucking neck.

"Oh, Gary. You really do seem to find yourself in situations that are going to get you killed," Dalton says cheerfully just as Dom practically rips the car door off its hinges.

Logan and Dalton act quickly, reaching in to drag Gary out as he struggles between them in a weak attempt to get away. Doesn't look like he's going anywhere unless he hobbles away with the cast on his broken leg. Courtesy of us throwing him out of his bedroom window. Good times.

"Start talking or else I'm cutting off your pickle dick and shoving it down your throat," Logan growls in Gary's paling face, and we all watch in disgust as a wet patch starts spreading over his pants.

"Seriously? That's just pathetic, man." Dalton gestures to

Gary's pants with a shake of his head, making a clicking noise with his tongue.

Gary whimpers, his eyes shifting around the parking lot, looking for an escape, but he might not even make it out alive. He makes eye contact with me, his wide eyes pleading, probably thinking I'm the weak link to get him out of this since I'm staying quiet and hanging back. I tilt my head, wondering...

"Did you watch them fuck?" I feel my upper lip curl and my hands twitching to snap his neck as sweat breaks out on his forehead.

"I–I woul–ld'nt do that!" Gary mumbles, avoiding my stare, which confirms the answer to my question.

"Why is your pulse racing then? I can smell your lies," Dom snarls in disgust, placing the end of his silencer under Gary's trembling chin, making his head tip back from the pressure of the barrel.

"It's not my fault they were fucking like rabbits in the school parking lot! That slut is nasty, man. The thing she did to your gearshift" The words coming out of his stupid mouth are cut off with a muffled pained shout the moment Dalton places his palm over Gary's mouth as I step forward and grasp his right hand, breaking his middle finger.

"Should have thrown you in an open grave and buried you alive when I had the chance. You got lucky, but it looks like that luck has run out." Logan gets up in Gary's face, his eyes flashing with so much anger that it makes me pause.

I think Tillie brings out the best in each of us, and not having her around is making us all go crazy. Logan and I are in for a world of pissed-off Tillie when we get her back. There's no way she doesn't know about Paris. I bet our girl gave that skank the bloody nose. If I have to tie Tillie up for her stubborn ass to hear us out, I will.

"Since you were being a pervert, you must have heard something when they were being kidnapped." Dalton cracks his big knuckles once after he takes his hand away from Gary's mouth, staring intently at him, watching him visibly swallow nervously.

"I don't know anything!" Gary's eyes start to water and I think we would be doing the world a favor getting rid of him.

"Yes, you do. Tell us now or your brain matter is going all over the window of your car," Dom threatens, nudging the gun more firmly under Gary's chin to let him know he's very serious.

"It's Larry's c–car." Gary whimpers as Logan lets out an impatient growl and holds his hand up, as if to hold back a very pissed-off Italian. "They were talking about some restaurant. Sounded Mexican! Loco something?" Gary looks at us hopefully, and for once, the fucker is useful.

"Why does that sound familiar?" Dalton asks, scratching the beard he's growing out.

"Loco Tacos. It's on the east side, right on the border of Carlos' territory." Dom pulls away, swearing rapidly in Spanish.

I stare at Logan as his whole body freezes. I don't think he's even breathing. My brain is running a mile a minute, already one step ahead as I plan on pulling up the restaurant layout online while changing all the red lights to green at every intersection on the way so we don't have to stop in traffic. This is gang business, which only means one thing, and I hate it.

"I have to call Jin," I mutter grimly and watch numbly as Logan suddenly punches Gary so hard that a tooth falls out and he collapses to the ground, knocked out cold.

"This day fucking sucks. Take this piece of trash back to

the club, I'll deal with him later," Dalton promises darkly, gesturing towards Gary before pulling off his biker vest and throwing it towards Axel, his vice president, as he starts barking at the guys to hurry the fuck up and get this mess cleaned up. They all scatter like their asses are on fire and Axel just salutes Dalton as he walks away to stand over the rest of the club members while tucking his president's vest away in his bike's saddle.

The vest can't go in a car. It's a biker rule.

He walks over to the idling Challenger and climbs in the front seat without even bothering to ask Dom if he minds. Dom just shoves his gun away and jogs over to his car, gunning the engine before he even has his door shut.

"You ready for this?" I grab the back of Logan's neck, making sure he's looking at me.

"If something happens to her..." he trails off, his nostrils flaring and eyes darkening.

"It won't. She's too pissed off at us to die. She knows," I say casually, letting go and rounding towards the passenger side of my car.

"Knows what?" Logan asks, looking at me over the top of the car roof.

"Paris."

Just that one name and Logan blanches.

Yeah. We're in deep shit.

Nothing like an angry woman to make you fear for your life.

CHAPTER 3

Tillie

My cheekbones hurt as Cruz squeezes them between his thumb and index fingers hard enough that my teeth and gums start to ache.

"It seems someone forgot their obedience lessons, haven't we? Don't worry, that will be fixed in no time." Cruz leans in closer, his gaze holding mine as he slowly starts to smile.

It's a smile that's not quite right. Crooked and practiced, like he really doesn't know how to feel any sense of happiness but enjoys my fear so much that some part of him deep inside is genuinely happy. I can't help shrinking away from him in fear, it's instinct. I hate that, letting him see that I'm still afraid. Seeing Tey out of the corner of my eye, his whole body vibrating with rage helps me steel my spine. I don't need to be scared of Cruz, he's just a man. Nothing more. I keep repeating that in my head until I stop shaking.

"You'll never have a piece of me again, Cruz. I'd rather die." I whip my head to the side, breaking his hold on my face.

"Hmm. You have changed. So fierce, pretending to be brave, but how brave will you be if I start hacking your boyfriend over here in pieces? How long will it take until you start begging for his life and give me what I want?" Cruz stands up, staring at me for a second before stepping in front of Tey.

Cold fear settles in my gut. I'll take any beating, look death in the eye without regret, but if he harms the men I love... I will just become a shell of myself.

"Bring it on, you mother trucker! I'm going to cut off your thumbs and shove them up your butthole. Rip off that pathetic dick and make it into a puppet before putting on a show for you as you slowly bleed to death," Tey says venomously, spitting at Cruz's dirty boots.

"I see. Death isn't a fear for you. What if I shove my dick in Tillie's ass while you watch? Her screams ringing in your ears for days as I take her again and again?" Cruz shakes his head and dismisses Tey, turning his back to him without a care in the world as Tey's icy-blue eyes drill holes in the back of his head with murderous intent.

My chest grows tight, but I try not to show any reaction as Cruz stares me down with his head tilted, the devious thoughts showing on his face the longer he looks at me.

He suddenly crouches in front of me and grasps my ankles, spreading my legs. I instantly start to fight back, kicking any body part of his I can reach. It's useless though as he kneels on my calves and grabs hold of the fist that isn't chained up when I started to swing at him.

"Last time you just laid there as your body was used again and again. Cried and screamed in pain. Have to say, you fighting back just gets me more excited." Cruz trails his hand up my inner thigh and pinches me so hard when I try to squeeze my legs closed.

"Don't give him what he wants, Tillie. Keep fighting. It just shows that you will never want him," Tey's voice is raspy and low, almost like he's choking. "How does that feel, Cruz, knowing she'll never want you? She spreads her legs wide open for me, like a flower blooming, begging for it."

What is he doing?! Cruz is going to kill Tey for taunting him. I can't take my gaze off Cruz with wide eyes, cringing as he slowly looks over at Tey with eyes full of such hate and rage.

"Shut up! Shut up!" Cruz hops off me and pulls out the knife that carved me up years ago.

He steps in Tey's direction with the knife raised but stops when the door bangs open. I can't stop screaming, the chain cutting into my wrist as I fight to stop him before he kills Tey right in front of me. I stare at Tey as if it's the last time I'll see him. I'd rather look at him if we're both going to die.

"Make the bitch stop with the shrieking. We have a problem." One of the goons cautiously steps into the room, his eyes shifty and not meeting Cruz's gaze when he looks at him over his shoulder.

My screams trail off and the ache in my chest fucking hurts. I thought this was it, the last time I would see those beautiful eyes of Tey staring at me. I'm panting as I slowly sit up, feeling like I've just woken from a nightmare. Sweat gathers at the back of my nape and my hands can't stop shaking, the chains slightly rattling.

"I'm busy. Handle it yourself." Cruz glances back down at Tey and cracks his neck from side to side.

"We have company. The rest of them are here for these two, and they didn't come alone." The tattooed gang member scratches the back of his neck with nerves.

"Fuck!" Cruz screams, tipping his head back and gripping his hair.

Holy shit.

I've never seen him lose it like this.

"Stay here with them. I'll be back." He points towards the gang member and starts walking to the door before glancing one more time at me. "We have so much to talk about. You've made so many mistakes, got so many people who cared about you killed, just because you wanted freedom from me. Diana, that trucker. *Tsk tsk,* little bird. Oh, can't forget about Rig. This isn't over, little bird," Cruz gloats with a sick glee while staring at me, as if he's waiting for me to open my mouth and ask about what I really want to know most, but I'm not giving him what he wants... not yet. "Not by a long shot." My lip curls as I glare at him until he's gone.

My whole body sags and tears gather at the corner of my eyes, not caring about the gang member seeing me breaking down.

"I'm proud of you, Tillie. You got some big lady balls on you." Tey catches my attention with how serious his tone is and makes a tearful giggle escape me. He scoots as close to me as he can and cups my face with his free hand, smoothing his thumb over my throbbing cheekbone. "Ready to play a game with me?" He whispers so low that it's hard to make out what he says before nodding his head towards the gang member leaning against the door looking bored as he picks at his nails.

"What do you need me to do?" I reply just as quietly, staring into his blue eyes that light up in excitement.

I know that look. Someone is bloodthirsty.

"Time to put those seductive moves to work." He winks and pulls away, sitting back like he's waiting for the show to begin.

If I imagine it's just me and him in here, I can do this. I've stripped naked in front of hundreds of men, one more isn't getting me killed. Just the unlucky gang member.

"Oh God. It's so hot in here," I say loudly and breathlessly. The gang member glances at me, raising a brow when he sees me staring at him. I squirm in place, tilting my head to the side and back so he can see the sweat dripping down my neck and into my shirt. "Tey. Can you take my bra off? I'm going to have a heatstroke." I turn to Tey, winking at him as I arch my back and pout.

"Sorry. My hand is chained. Can't help you, but maybe he can?" Tey shrugs and glances away, like he's disinterested in the whole matter.

"Please? My bra is getting wet with the sweat dripping down between my boobs, and I need air to cool off," I whine while turning towards the gang member, looking up at him from under my lashes.

"Yeah, bitch. I can do that." He grins cockily and swaggers over to me with heat in his eyes as he stares down at my heaving breasts.

Sucker.

He kneels in front of me and reaches behind me, his fingers fumbling with the clasp. Before he can unhook one, Tey quickly leans back and wraps his strong calves around the guy's neck. I act without thinking, moving just as fast to get my legs around his waist to hold him still and trapping his arms. Tey grunts and shifts his legs so fast that I almost miss it, but the loud crack of bone snapping sends a shiver down my spine.

I stare at the gang member, releasing him the instant he dies, then look over at Tey to see him grinning proudly from snapping someone's neck like a twig.

"You scare me sometimes, you know that?" I mutter and shake my head, but I can't help it when my lips stretch into a smile as he blows a kiss at me.

"Wouldn't have it any other way, baby. Be a doll and hand me that gun on his hip." He jerks his chin to the gun tucked into the gang member's pants. Pulling it out, I wordlessly hand it over to Tey and watch as he points the barrel at the chain wrapped around the pole. "Look away," he warns before firing the shot just as I turn my head. My ears ring from how close the gunshot was. Tey quickly stands up, the cuff of the chain still wrapped around his wrist, but at least he's not chained to the pole anymore. "Your turn." He stands next to my shoulder and presses my head into his thigh to muffle the sound of the gun. The moment my wrist is free, it drops into my lap, numb from being held up for so long. I stand on shaking legs and grip Tey's bicep, feeling like I need a bath and a long nap. "Let's get out of here. If my guess is correct, the guys are here and they won't be leaving without us." Tey wraps an arm around my waist and leads me to the door with a slight limp in his step.

"Wait. You guess? How do you not know if we're walking to our deaths?" I look up at him with a frown, hating seeing his bruised face.

"Life is always a guess and every footstep you take forward eventually leads to your death," he states matter-of-factly with a shrug before looking around the doorway real quick, glancing both ways to make sure the coast is clear.

"You're so full of shit, but for some reason, that makes me feel better." I roll my eyes and stick to his side like glue as we step out into a hallway leading to stairs that go up.

"I'm all about the feels, my sweet cherry pie." He places a chaste kiss on the side of my forehead as we quietly walk up the stairs, the smell of food getting stronger and music with the sound of voices rising.

"This may not be the epic death you hoped for like the Titanic, but it could be a dramatic, bloody shoot-out. Till death do us part?" I whisper into his ear, smirking as he shivers.

"Fuck. Guess I have to live since you just, ya know, married us. I do, by the way." He chuckles darkly and tightens his fingers on my hip just as we bust through the door at the top of the stairs without any warning.

It would seem we stumbled into a party. Well, it's more like Logan pointing his gun at Cruz, who just stands there doing nothing as if it doesn't bother him that he has a gun held to his head. It doesn't. Sociopaths don't care about death, they feel nothing. Carlos is glancing around, probably looking for a way out, like the coward he is, and then there's Jin, who's calmly sitting at a table and watching everything unfold with a hint of glee in his eyes.

I hope he's the first to get shot.

CHAPTER 4

Logan

"How much longer?" I grip the steering wheel, taking a deep breath to stay calm, but it's not helping.

For the first time ever, I have this rising panic, a thick weight in my chest, thinking that we aren't going to get there in time. What if we're too late? What if we walk into Loco and both of them are already dead?

Fuck. I feel my harsh breath rushing faster and faster out of my mouth as my thoughts swirl. I place my gun on my lap before I end up shooting one of us by pulling the trigger accidentally while driving like a maniac.

"Turn left. Two minutes out," Nicky says in a robotic voice, but I can hear the tightness in his tone.

He's not doing so good either. We all aren't.

I press my foot down harder on the gas pedal and turn sharply left, shifting the sticky gear shift to speed up. I don't even care that Tillie and Tey's cum is on my hand, or her blood. I just want them back. Nicky slams his computer shut, throwing it in the backseat without caring where it lands, and opens the glove compartment to hand me a gun while he takes one for himself.

"I messaged Jin. He's already there. Apparently, he was in the neighborhood." Nicky shifts his gaze towards me, our eyes communicating to not say what we're really thinking out loud.

We need to check all the cars and our houses for bugs. There's no way Jin just happened to be in the east side neighborhood. He's either listening in or having someone watching us. Fuck. I quickly change the subject just in case.

"Are you sure she knows about Paris?" I grind my teeth together, knowing she's going to jump to conclusions and not trust a damn word out of my mouth.

I can't blame her. We all don't trust easily, and however she found out what Nicky and I were up to... it's going to look bad.

"Well, I saw Paris today and she looked like she had been through a blender. My guess is Tillie beat the shit out of her. Not surprising really. It was only a matter of time since Paris thinks she sits on a pedestal and loves to make everyone feel beneath her, especially our girl. Paris is obsessed with you too. Did you see this turning out any other way? We should have told Tillie, but no. You didn't want to involve her, and now it's blowing up in our face." Nicky shakes his head in disgust as he leans over, throwing his Glock in the glove compartment in anger, and clenches his pants legs in his fists as he sits back.

"You're right." I heave out a breath. I can't believe how much I fucked up. "I promised her no more secrets, and I already screwed it up because of my pride. I just want to keep everyone I care about safe!" I shout, suddenly punching the steering wheel, thanks to all the raging emotions and guilt bubbling up inside of me.

I see the sign of the Mexican restaurant down the block

and try to gain some of my control back. It has to work out. She'll have to forgive me once she knows everything.

"You about done? Get your head on straight. Besides, if she really thought we cheated on her... she would have killed us or left instead of having sex in my car with Tey. They both know I can't stand messes, but this kind of mess, I really don't mind. I would love to paint both of them in my cum, soaking into their skin so they smell like me for days. That's the kind of mess I want." Nicky checks the bullet chamber, clicking it back into place, and acting like he didn't just admit something out loud that's never easy for him.

Tillie is really changing us all for the better.

Nicky is starting to not give a shit about what Jin thinks.

Tey is letting his psycho fly and loving life.

Dalton's rough edges have calmed down, as if he's found peace with this life.

I... Nothing else matters to me except my family. The people who aren't blood but all the same. They're my brothers and the woman who makes my cold heart beat again.

"I'm proud of you, Nicholas." Just saying the words feels as though they were ripped from my soul, but the minute they were out, I felt a weight lift off my shoulders.

"Shit. Don't start getting emotional on me now. Our people are in that building. Be the Logan who we need, then afterwards you can go back to being a sap." I turn my head to see Nicky wiping away the smirk that just formed on his face.

Looking back at the road, I pull into the restaurant's parking lot and slam on the brakes so hard that we jerk forward in our seats. I don't bother turning off the engine, better to leave it running, just in case. Stepping out, I flex my stiff fingers around the trigger of my gun and straighten my suit as I quickly take in our surroundings. Jin's freaking limo is already in the parking lot, and Dom's car is parked closer to the back of the restaurant.

Good. Both exits will be watched if shit hits the fan. It's one thing me and Dom have in common; taking over a situation without hesitation and looking at all outcomes.

Nicky gets out of the car and looks over at me with a perfectly raised black eyebrow once he notices I'm already looking at him.

"I'm going in alone," I say, noticing his jaw tightening at the order.

"No." His lip curls, breaking out of his stoic facial expression.

"No? You're going to lose your cool walking in there, seeing Jin treating this like a business meeting. You know I'm right. I'm going to get them out of there," I promise him, seeing the indecision in his gaze until he kicks his tire and rounds to the trunk.

"Fine, but the moment anything goes south, I'm coming in guns blazing. The moment we learn the truth of everything, Lo, I'm done holding back," Nicky vows, opening the trunk to pull out a rifle under a hidden compartment.

"We'll all have that day very soon." I slap him on the shoulder and head towards the entrance of the restaurant without looking back.

The moment I enter the building, the smell of cooked meat and loud, upbeat Mexican music hits my senses all at once. If this place wasn't a hangout for dipshit fuckers, I'd eat here on a taco Tuesday. The atmosphere is low lighting and family-oriented. Too bad it's all just a front for gang members to hang out. We should really blow this place up, just because.

I scan the seating area, looking at families sitting in

booths and eating without a care in the world, not knowing that any minute someone could draw a gun and it ends up being a shoot-out. I spot the back of Jin's head near the rear of the restaurant in a dark corner, sitting at a table, and across from him sits Carlos.

I walk over to them slowly, like I have all the time in the world, and try to keep my facial expression clear of any emotions. Carlos glances over Jin's head and smirks, raising his tequila glass at me before throwing it back.

"Logan. What brings you to my neighborhood, cholo?" Carlos asks innocently and gestures for me to take a seat next to Jin, but I stay standing instead.

Like hell I'm going to sit at a dining table with him. My mother always said a kitchen table is where friends and family gather.

"Let's cut to the chase, shall we? I have places to be. Where are they?" My eyes bore into his, waiting for him to look away first.

"Logan, where are your manners? Didn't know Franco raised an animal." Jin speaks up for the first time since I got here, glancing over his shoulder at me as he grabs a handkerchief out of his suit pocket and starts wiping down the table in front of him like it's dirty.

"Apologies, Jin. How are you?" It takes everything in me to not spit the words at him, but my voice comes out sincere and pleasant as I turn my head to look at him.

"Good, good. Just having a business meeting, although I expected my son to be here." He doesn't look at me as he talks, a sign of disrespect, and Carlos is eating it all up.

"He's busy doing some gun inventory with Dalton at the moment." I smile wide and walk around the table to the other side so Jin can see me.

"Shame." Jin grinds out, absolutely not pleased that he

didn't get his way. "Carlos was just telling me that he wants to make a deal, but I haven't decided if it's worth it. Why don't you share, boy?" Jin still hasn't looked at me and I know it's intentional to act like he sees me as someone who isn't important.

Fuck him.

Carlos' smile gets tight around the edges at the boy comment, but he leans back in his chair in a slouched position to appear like he's unbothered.

"I found two strays that you could sell in your auction... for a price, of course." Carlos lazily flicks out a cigarette and lights the tip, blowing the smoke towards me.

"I have plenty of merchandise, why would I be interested, as you say, in *strays*? Isn't one of them Nicholas' pet, Logan?" Jin glances at me with a sly smile, clearly already knowing the answer and trying to rile me up.

"No idea. Though I'm sure Franco would be upset to learn his stepdaughter was being traded like cattle with a lower drug dealer from the hood. Really? What is the world coming to?" I gesture to Carlos with a nonchalant shrug, noticing him sitting up straighter out of the corner of my eye as I disrespect him on his turf.

"You fucking Italians think you're so much better than anyone else. I'm going to pop a cap in your ass." Carlos stands up, his chair falling to the ground along with his cigarette, but he doesn't notice as he leans over the table to get in my face.

"Carlos," a deep voice snaps from behind me, making my shoulders stiffen at being exposed. "These are your guests, no? How about a fair trade? To show our respect to the triad and the police chief by protecting his precious stepdaughter, we can leave them in your hands."

I slowly turn around, trying hard not to pull my gun out

and shoot this fucking biker in the head and balls. A Demon Jokers patch rests right over his breast pocket, the black leather of his vest worn and used with wrinkles. I stare into his dead, blue eyes and have a cold feeling sweep through my body. His dirty blond hair is unkempt, greasy, and long, hanging down over his wide shoulders. He's just about as tall as me and his muscles are just as built. Everything else about him screams off, like a body without a soul. You only have to look into someone's eyes and see their thoughts. Even Nicky, the one person I know who can turn off his emotions like a switch, has a tell that he still feels things. It's the way his eyes look deep into your own, accessing what kind of human you are.

This fucker in front of me... I get nothing. His stare is so blank, his face so relaxed that I can't tell what he's thinking.

"What?! I'm not giving—" Carlos starts to yell, slamming his palm on the table, but Jin cuts him off.

"How very generous of you. A businessman, I see. That we have in common. You have my interest, what do you want in return?" Jin asks, intrigued as he gives his full attention to the biker, eyeing him with respect, and Carlos just huffs in annoyance as he sits his ass back down.

Fuck.

"Drugs. Selling, running them on the streets, getting them into the hands of lowlifes and teenagers to feed their future addiction. We want in. Demon Jokers already trade in cocaine. Why not work together, and Carlos' gang can come in handy, having more of his people on the streets." This fucker lights a cigarette and holds Jin's stare with a crooked grin that looks fake as shit.

"I could always use more people to run my product." Jin ponders before standing up and reaching to shake the biker's hand. "I didn't get your name?"

"Cruz," he says as he clasps Jin's hand in a firm shake before letting go to turn towards me but I stop him from moving.

He doesn't even blink as I whip out my gun without thinking about the consequences and put it to his temple. Images of him hurting my baby girl, touching her, and raping her with other bikers flips through my mind at rapid speed. He's the one who broke her, before me and the guys came along to pick up the pieces. Just the thought of his dirty fingernails on her beautiful skin has my hand trembling, making it obvious that my emotions are all over the place as the gun shakes slightly in my grip.

"Do I know you?" Cruz says without even trying to defend himself, turning to look at the barrel now between his eyebrows. I don't notice anything else around me, it's only me and this fucker. I'll kill him.

"No, but you're about to," I grind out through my teeth, digging my gun harder into his skin.

"Now, now, boy. What would Franco say to this behavior? Put the gun away, Logan," Jin orders, sounding amused before he turns back towards Cruz to address him. "We are having an auction Thursday at the docks PointCross starting at nine o'clock at night. Why don't you join us so we can all discuss business and give you a chance to meet Franco?"

My finger tightens on the trigger, seconds away from shooting Cruz in the fucking face.

"Carlos and I would be honored. Wouldn't miss it for the world," Cruz replies, holding my gaze and puffing smoke into my face.

"Logan, put the gun down." Tillie's soft voice reaches my ears, bringing me out of the static and ringing that was pounding in my eardrum.

I don't lower the gun, not breaking my stare with this

fucker as he looks over to the right. There it is. Emotion. Cruz's neck starts to turn red, the vein on his forehead pulsing, but the look in his gaze actually terrifies me. I see someone who looks at something as an object, wanting to keep it locked up and away from everyone except himself.

Obsession.

Greed.

Ownership.

Over my dead fucking body.

"Mine." My voice comes out menacing and deep, making no mistake about what the fuck I mean.

Tillie is mine, not fucking his.

Cruz whips his gaze away from Tillie, staring at me with a snarl on his face as he steps closer, the reek of his breath stinging my nostrils. He doesn't say anything while he brings his hand up and stabs the burnt end of his cigarette onto the collar of my white shirt. I grit my teeth, embracing the burning pain seeping into my skin, and smirk when he notices he won't get the reaction he's looking for. The scars on my back from being beaten over and over by a belt through the years proves that I can feel nothing when I shut off my mind.

"Little bird escapes her cage again, but what will happen when I clip off those wings you love to spread?" Cruz flicks his cigarette, turning his head to stare at what's mine.

"Eyes on me. You don't get to look at her," I growl, about to shoot him in the head before a soft touch pulls me out of my rage of vengeance killing.

"He's not yours to kill, Logan. I want to leave, please," Tillie whispers in my ear, standing at my shoulder as she strokes her thumb over the top of my hand holding the gun.

She's right. I know this, but the urge to just end this waste of space is so strong. He doesn't deserve to live.

"Well! This has been entertaining, gentleman, but I have places to be. Cruz, Carlos, we'll see you Thursday." Jin claps his hands together, standing up as he buttons his suit jacket and squeezes my shoulder as he passes by me. "I'll be in touch with Franco. Don't worry, boy, I'll tell him all about today."

To anyone else, he would sound helpful, but he knows just how mad Franco is going to be when he finds out I went into gang territory without him, causing a scene in a family restaurant, and showing my emotion for Tillie.

I don't watch Jin leave, or the men in black suits that seem to come out of the shadows to follow him. Will those in the Triad follow Nicky like that too when Jin isn't around anymore? We can only fucking hope.

"Bro, we need to leave. Now," Tey demands, slapping Carlos hard on the back as he passes by, almost causing the gang leader to topple out of his seat. "Good seeing you, Carlos! What service! I'll give the restaurant a review on Yelp lata."

"I'll be seeing you real soon, little bird," Cruz promises, not once taking his stare off her as she tugs on my arm and gets me to slowly lower my gun.

"Can't wait," she says in a strong voice. I wish I could see her face, but I don't want to take my gaze off Cruz until I know she's safe.

I push Tillie behind me, seeing Tey out of the corner of my eye come over to lead her towards the front of the restau-rant with his hands on the small of her back. The whole place is silent and I'm wondering if everyone left when I pulled out my gun, or the moment I reached their table if they could feel the tension in the air. I know the moment she's left the building as Cruz glances back over at me and just stares with dead, frigid eyes.

"Just remember this to help you sleep better at night. I had that juicy ass first. Her screams are mine." Cruz has the last word before he walks away and grabs Carlos' collar to drag him into the kitchen.

I don't waste time, quickly leaving and banging through the front entrance with my gaze swinging everywhere for her. I briefly catch Jin talking to Nicky as he disassembles the rifle and puts it back in the trunk of his car. The moment his attention is back on his father, Jin slaps him so hard on the cheek that his head whips to the side. Nicky licks his lip as he slowly looks back at Jin, his eyes cold and his whole body stiff with pent-up rage. I don't hear what Jin's saying to Nicky, but I do know there will be hell to pay for both of us. Jin takes off after that, getting into his limo as Nicky stares at me from across the back of the car before he looks over at the back of the building, off to the right. Looking over, I see Tillie wrapped up in Dom's suit jacket and being cuddled into Dalton's arms as he strokes her hair. He whispers something in her ear and passes her to Dom, who sweeps her up into his arms and strides over to his car before placing her in the front seat. Tey says something to Dalton then jogs over to Nicky and I. If I had the energy, I'd be rolling my eyes at his peach underwear, but I can't even crack a smile. Dom drives by, nodding his head as he starts to pull into traffic. My eyes connect with Tillie's for a split second, but all I see is hurt and pain before she dismisses me.

"You both have some explaining to do. You're lucky I've known you fuckers for a long time. You hurt her. She knows about Paris, Lo. Your favorite journalist did an article about you guys online at Dom's club with her." Tey blows a raspberry and shakes his head in disappointment as he stares at Nicky.

Nicky kicks his tire and gets into the car, slamming the door behind him.

"Shit." I run my hand through my hair before getting into the passenger side as I call myself an idiot over and over again for fucking up the one goddamn good thing in my life.

"Yup!" Tey states cheerfully, popping the P as he gets in the backseat and leans forward over the console. "So, somebody better start talking before my feelings get hurt and I get stabby. Who has my unicorn, by the way? I'm having withdrawals."

I hate this day.

CHAPTER 5

Tillie

Sometimes I wish life would throw me a whole fucking lemon tree and then my glass would never go empty. In a way, I would have been ignorant of the wrongs in the world, so much hate and violence hidden away from me. It could have seemed like I lived in a bubble, protected, but I'm shit out of luck.

I want to scream, cry, and rage that it's not fair the life I've been dealt. As if my being created was a gamble, just a roll of the dice that ended up on the losing side. I've lived in despair and woe is me. I could have it a lot worse. Being human trafficked by Jin and sold to who knows where. Then again, I'd probably take those chances than ever having to be near Cruz again.

God.

Cruz.

I can't believe I was breathing the same air as him, having him so dreadfully close to me. It really was pure luck that I'm still in one piece right now, but for how long? Cruz has to know about the guys and me. There was no hiding that, and now my worst fear is becoming a reality. I've brought so much danger to their door and put their lives at risk. It's all my fault if anything happens to them. I do wonder how much it takes before a person loses their sanity from having everything thrown at them at once. How the hell am I still functioning? I should just give myself over before my mind splits in half and I end up getting my guys killed.

I think I'm going to be sick.

I feel stuck all of a sudden and the urge to run is very, very strong, as if the car doors on either side are closing in on me. I'm seconds away from opening the door, not caring how fast it's going, and taking a fucking leap out. Either into Cruz's grasp to get it all over with or far, far away that Tillie no longer exists.

"Stop. Don't go there, little bitch. Get out of your fucking head or I'll make you." Dalton leans between the two front seats and wraps the palm of his hand around my throat, using his thumb on my chin to turn my head towards him. "If you even think about running, I'll chase after you and chain you to my bed. You get me?" The intensity of his violent gaze burns into mine with so much understanding and a promise to follow through with keeping me in his sights, even if it involves shackling my wrists in metal. How does he do that? He always seems to know when I'm on the verge of freaking out and having a meltdown. Holding his gaze, I swallow harshly around his hand and give him a tiny nod. "Good girl. There's nothing we can do at this very moment, so sit back and enjoy the fucking ride." He grips the pulsing pressure points on either side of my neck and gently skims his fingers along my skin as he lets go.

"You're such a dick." My voice comes out husky as I furrow my brows at how much I miss the warmth of his hand around my throat.

"You like my big dick," he grumbles and sits back in his

seat, taking up the whole space back there with his broad shoulders.

I shake my head and lean against the headrest, closing my eyes instead of looking out the windows. Honestly, I don't care where we're going as long as it puts them out of reaching distance from Cruz. That's all I care about. I love Dalton, Tey, Dom, and even Nicky and Logan for some sick, fucked up reason. They're in a world of pain when I see them again. I'm going to twist off Logan's balls for hurting me.

"Sit tight, Mama. We're almost to my place. You'll be safe there," Dom rasps in that smokey voice of his, his hand snaking around my upper thigh and squeezing.

For the rest of the ride, he doesn't move his hand, just softly rubs his thumb back and forth in a gesture that slowly relaxes my body with the soft purr of his car, making me start to drift off.

I feel the car slow down ten minutes later and the sound of something buzzing followed by a soft squeak has me opening my eyes. A towering, solid metal door slides open on the driveway, letting Dom through the moment enough space is available for the car to fit. I look in the rearview mirror, watching the gate close, and breathe easier when I see the tall, cement walls surrounding the whole place. Dom's house is like a fortress, I wouldn't be surprised if he had a moat. He cuts off the engine and the only sound meeting my ears is of our breathing filling the car.

"Damn." Dalton whistles from the backseat before getting out with his hands on his hips as he stares up at the mansion in front of us.

It's like something out of a movie; beautiful and classy. With a clay tile roof, it seems to have the Mediterranean vibe, and the house structure is tan like sand with bright green vines of pink and red blooming flowers crawling up the walls. It's very homey and classical with palm trees surrounding the outside. I feel like I've stepped into Spain with all the vivid, lush colors that have a calming effect and charm.

"Dom, it's exquisite," I breathe out and soak it all in, shuddering as he buttons up the jacket over my shoulders so I'm not freezing while standing in his driveway.

"You should see the house in Mexico. All in good time, Mama. Let's get you inside and I'll give you a tour later." Dom guides me up the steps with his hand on my lower back, practically holding me up as exhaustion eats away at me.

The front door opens before we make it up to the last step. A short, sweet, little old lady stands there with a blossoming smile as she reaches up and clasps Dom's cheeks.

He has to bend down as she places a kiss on each cheek and pinches him. My brows raise at the slight pink covering his cheekbones.

"*Nieto*! You are getting too thin. I'll make you some Arroz Cubano." She fits over Dom, clicking her tongue before turning to Dalton and I with an equally warm smile. "Such sad eyes, but don't fear, *Mija*, my Dom will make you a very happy wife."

I nearly choke on my tongue and smack Dalton's chest as he coughs into his fist in amusement.

"*Yaya*! Let her inside before you scare her away," Dom mutters in exasperation, gesturing for his grandmother to walk ahead of us.

"Don't worry, *Mija*, he loves me, and you won't have to worry about me walking in on any lovemaking. I want grandbabies. I'm not getting any younger, *Nietos*. I live in the guesthouse in the back of the property for my own space.

Feel free to come visit me when you're not working on giving me a great grandchi—" his grandmother gushes excitedly until Dom cuts her off, and I already know he's in for a world of hurt for interrupting her, I can see it in her face that's laced with displeasure.

"Enough, *Yaya*." Dom winces as his grandmother suddenly has her slipper in her hand and starts whacking him on the shoulder with it. "Jesus. I'm sorry! Tillie, Dalton, this is my lovely grandmother, Isabella." Dom gestures to both of us when his grandmother stops smacking him and he clasps my hand, rubbing his thumb back and forth on my wrist.

"It's very nice to meet you." I sound like a dying frog, my throat dry as I sway on my feet.

"Ma'am," Dalton says with respect. He stands on my other side as he wraps his arm around my waist to hold me up, not caring that he's boxing me in between him and Dom.

"I'll get started on dinner while you go rest, you look dead on your feet, child." She pats my cheek affectionately with a knowing look as she glances at Dom and Dalton standing on either side of me protectively.

I just nod my head with a small smile and sag against Dalton as she walks briskly into a kitchen near the back of the house. I'm suddenly being swung up into a pair of strong arms and cradled against a warm chest as I nuzzle my face into Dom's neck. He starts walking, carrying me farther into his house, and I glance over his shoulder to make sure Dalton is following. His eyes meet mine, those kissable lips of his curling at the edge as I reach over Dom's shoulder with one arm and trail my fingertips over the light scruff on Dalton's sharp jawline. He mouths, *"Love you,"* and it makes my heart skip a beat.

I can't believe we went from enemies to freaking lovers, not trusting and practically at each other's throats to this insane love that feels like it can last forever. Does it make me fucked up that I love all their rough edges and want to bring out the darkest side of each of them? I think back to that night in the garage as they loomed over me, forcing me to my knees and fucking my mouth until my lips were swollen and red. I stare at Dalton now and I want him as he is, even when he shoves his big cock down my throat like he owns me. He does, but I own him too. I like all the sides that are cut and sharp to the touch, but the soft side they only let me see makes my insides melt too.

It's confusing as hell, but that's me.

At some point, we enter a room, but Dom strides through it too fast for me to really look at it. He flicks on a light and slowly sets me down right next to the shower glass door. Without a word, he turns on the water with his hand outstretched under the spray until it's to his liking. It better be scorching hot or else I don't want it.

I kind of stand there in a daze, swaying on my feet as I watch the glass door fog up. Hands sweeping my hair away from my breastbone makes me jump a little until I feel the soft touch of lips on my neck and the scruff of Dalton's beard leaving behind a slight burn.

"Let us take care of you, and after, sleep. No talking about anything that happened today, okay?" Dalton whispers against my skin, grabbing the labels of Dom's jacket around my shoulders from behind and easing it away until it drops onto the tiled floor.

Dom steps forward and gets to one knee in front of me, kissing my stomach as he draws down my underwear. He glances back up at me, his gaze flickering between Dalton and I with a look I can't understand. Content, maybe?

Relaxed? I don't know, but I wasn't expecting them to get along so well.

"Okay." My voice comes out soft, afraid speaking any louder will break this intimate moment between us.

I can't help but stroke my index finger along Dom's dark brow and watch as his eyes close at my touch, his face relaxing, as if he's been strung too tight this whole time. I'm standing naked in front of both men after Dalton unsnaps my bra within seconds, yet I don't get the feeling this is about sex. Of course, the sexual tension is there. I'm naked, but both guys are handling me like I'm fragile and precious. It's such a strange feeling, one that's going to take a long time getting used to.

Dom climbs to his feet, stripping out of his clothes and exposing golden skin with each item of clothing he drops to the floor. I'm only human, so I let my gaze slide over his body. He has big, tan feet, muscular calves with hair that I want to feel rubbing against my legs, thick thighs that could squeeze a watermelon open, and the perfect place to park my ass on. My eyes linger on his cock, watching it twitch the longer I stare. He's so fucking long and thick... He's not even hard. Jesus. I can't believe that thing slid down my throat. I could have suffocated to death. My gaze keeps moving, pretty sure I'm hardcore eye fucking him and not caring one bit. Why do the indents of a man's hip have to be so damn sexy? It instantly draws my gaze there, and it's like a leading arrow forcing your gaze to go lower. My eyes continue devouring him and I note that his abs are stacked and tight, making my mouth water. If I lick it, then it's mine, right? His biceps are huge, and it makes me want to be cuddled against him just as much as I want to drape myself over his perfectly broad shoulders.

I hear the rustling of Dalton behind me before I feel his

hot, naked skin against my back as he hooks his arm around my waist and lifts me up like I weigh nothing.

"You're lucky I'm not a self-conscious man. The way you were just staring at him reminds me of setting a plate of chocolate cake in front of you. The same look you always give me." Dalton sets me down under the hot water and turns me in his arms until I'm looking up at him.

"You guys and chocolate cake are equally the loves of my life," I joke, leaning into him with a small smile before it drops.

Loving these guys is hard, even when I want to leave Logan and hurt him just as much as he's hurt me, but the heart wants what it wants. It sucks, the back-and-forth way my head and heart go at each other.

Head: "Leave his ass."

Heart: "But we love him for some stupid reason."

"No thinking, Mama. Just feel. We're going to wash the day away from you, and you're going to let us," Dom states, leaving no room for argument, but he won't hear any complaints from me.

Fingers weave into my hair, smoothing the wet strands with shampoo before scrubbing gently at my scalp. Is there such a thing as a hair-wash orgasm? Dalton starts washing my body slowly as I lean my back into Dom and close my eyes.

"Just a little bit longer, Tillie," Dalton mutters, not lingering on my breasts as he washes me, working his way down my body before dropping to his knees to wash my legs.

They're both really caring for me, and that makes my eyes well up with tears.

"You look good on your knees down there." I try to

lighten the mood, running my hand through his hair as he looks up at me with a lopsided smile.

"Wouldn't want to be anywhere else," he vows with a deep grumble in his voice, squeezing my hips before standing and hugging me to his chest as Dom finishes washing the conditioner from my hair.

"You own us, Tillie. It came out of nowhere, fast and hot enough to set the world on fire. I think we would do just about anything for you, even fucking Russo," Dom says passionately, stepping up to my back to sandwich me between their bodies, which are giving off enough heat that it warms me from the inside out.

"I know. I know this, but my mind isn't ready to think about everything right now," I mutter into Dalton's hard pec, letting my lips kiss his smooth skin.

"Tomorrow," Dom promises and nuzzles my neck.

"Tomorrow," I reply. Just being here in this moment, that doesn't hurt.

I can hurt tomorrow.

Dom

I didn't sleep last night because I couldn't take my eyes off of Tillie. My skin tightened in fear at just the thought of her disappearing on me, never seeing her again. I've never been a man that fears much, but the thought of waking up one day and Tillie not being here... it makes my heart race in terror. It also makes me want to destroy everything that could harm her and kill anyone that looks at her sideways. I'm only twenty-four years old, but with this worry about her life, I'll be lucky to make it to thirty.

"The guys are blowing up my phone. I'm giving them your address, and I would expect them to be here within an hour or less," Dalton grumbles into Tillie's neck, shifting closer to her back and taking a deep breath of her intoxicating scent before pulling away.

I understand the feeling.

"I already figured. We can't seem to stay away from her, can we?" I ask him but stare down at Tillie's sleeping face, smoothing out her furrowed brow with the tip of my finger.

What are you dreaming about, Mama, to cause such stress in your sleep?

"I have to say, I didn't see her coming, but I can't not see her in my life," Dalton says, heaving a big sigh before unwrapping his arms from around her and quietly climbing out of my bed. She doesn't wake but scoots closer to me, burrowing her face into my neck and throwing her thigh over my hip. Her hot breath warms my neck and I squeeze her more into my side, never wanting to go anywhere that she isn't. "I'm going to see if I can find some coffee and food for her. She gets hangry in the morning." Dalton chuckles, pulling on his shirt and looking back once more like he's tempted to climb back into bed with her, but instead, shakes his head while walking out of my bedroom.

I can't help but laugh softly under my breath because I'm the one who gets to hold my queen for a little longer. This is what peace feels like. Having her in my house, warming my bed, right by my side, just as the sun is rising.

I want this every morning.

Tillie, at that moment, lets out a groan and takes a deep inhale against my neck while running her soft hand up and down the hard muscles of my stomach. My cock has been hard all night, aching desperately to fill my queen with every single inch. It pulses and twitches with her exploring hands, but I ignore it because she doesn't need me jumping her like a starved man.

Even when I've never been hungrier.

"How do you smell so good? I bet you're the type of man who doesn't have morning breath," Tillie mumbles with a raspy voice before pulling back to look me in the eyes.

Her hair is a disheveled mess around her face as she squints her brown eyes, turning them a light brown with the sunlight shining through the windows.

"You're magnificent, Mama," I breathe out, taken by her beauty and in awe of how this woman is in my bed.

"Stop! It's too early for your smooth-talking." She groans but leans down to kiss my pec with a small smile.

"How are you feeling?" I ask softly, swiping the hair out of her eyes, and pushing it behind her ear as she glances under her lashes at me.

"Honestly?" She chews her lip, as if she's worried about whatever's on her mind.

"Always." I hold her stare, letting her know she can tell me anything and I'll never think less of her.

"I'm so angry... No, I'm furious. If you handed me a gun right now, you wouldn't be able to stop me from charging headfirst into the lion's den. I'll kill all those gang members and leave Cruz for last, just to make his death very fucking slow." Tillie's gaze burns with a fiery passion, her nails digging into my stomach before she blows out a frustrated breath. "I'm also hungry and horny. Unbelievably horny."

"Yes, to everything," I promise her, loving how her eyes grow wide as I clasp my hands under her arms and pull her fully on top of me.

I grunt as her warm pussy settles right over my stiff cock, only a thin layer separating us. Her lips part, eyes dilating, and her hair creates a curtain around us that blocks out everything else except me and her.

"You going to make me feel good, Papi?" she purrs, ghosting her soft lips along my jaw as her hand grips my throat in a possessive hold until my head tips back and she bites down on my chin.

"Don't you know by now, Mama? I'd give you anything. Name it and it's yours." I clench her ass in my hands, squeezing both cheeks and massaging as she lets out a low moan.

"Can you make me forget for a little while? Give me that, please? I feel like I'll die if I don't have you inside me right now," she confesses as she rocks her pussy over my hard cock, making it almost painful.

I don't think I've ever been this hard before. It's like all my blood has rushed straight to my cock, leaving my head empty for once. All I want is to feel her soft skin gliding against mine, her sweet scent the only thing I can breathe in. In the past, I would have been already pounding into the woman without any questions, but this is my queen. She's been through too much shit, and I don't want her to think all I want from her is sex. I'll cuddle her, worship at her feet if she wants, and give her anything she needs while ignoring my raging cock that's demanding to slide into her heat. When a man knows that he's found the one, the woman that fits into his side like a puzzle piece while feeling complete, he can wait a lifetime for her, as long as she ends up with my name on her skin in the end. I look into her beautiful, brown gaze and can see coming home to her every night, those pain-filled eyes shifting into happiness that I intend to make sure stays there. Women have come and gone, I'm not a saint, but not one of them compares to Tillie. Not one.

"I don't want to hurt you—" I start to say, stroking my thumb along her cheekbone, but she cuts me off with a hard shake of her head.

"You won't. Dom, I want you. It's that simple. If we met in another world, one that wasn't filled with violence, I'd still be here. Right where I'm supposed to be." She bites my bottom lip and tugs but lets out a yelp as I flip our position until I'm on top.

"I'm going to love you, Tillie. I'll give you everything, even when you don't know what you need. You're my fucking queen, and I know who's going to be warming my bed at night. It's always going to be you." My voice comes out gruff, every ounce of my being on fire for this feisty, passionate woman.

She grips my hair, yanking my head down until our lips crash together in a kiss that could set the bed on fire. My lips glide over hers as I grab her thigh, giving it a squeeze before pulling her leg up and over, right above my ass. She makes pleased little whimpers as I kiss the corner of her luscious lips, slowly dragging my tongue to the indent in the middle of her lips and biting down. The moment she gasps, I slide my tongue past her parted lips and stroke along hers with little flicks. I'm basically fucking her mouth, the same way I'm going to fuck her sweet pussy.

"Dom," she moans, rocking her hips up to rub against my cock, making me grit my teeth at how good her warm, wet pussy feels.

Her eyes drift down, lips parted as she looks between us to see my cock slipping out from the top of my black boxers. Only a thin layer separates me from plunging into her slick pussy. I groan, leaning my forehead against hers as we watch her panties grow wetter and wetter after each slide of my cock. The fabric has a very dark, wet spot of blood, and I can see her pussy lips sticking to the damp material. I'm practically salivating to be inside her.

"If it's not your thing when I'm on my period—" My head whips up and her cheeks instantly turn a blush pink.

"Not my thing? Mama, I'll suck the fucking soul out of your pretty pussy, blood and all." I grin wickedly, watching her eyes dilate once more and widen with desire.

I lean back on my haunches between her silky, parted thighs, starting to tug down the boxers I loaned her last night until her hand stops me. My eyes drag up from her perfectly pink pussy lips, connecting with her suddenly shy gaze. She bites her bottom lip until it's red and I'm intrigued with where her thoughts are as I stroke my thumb over her hip bone, trying to soothe her.

"Dom..." she says in a breathless sigh and stares up at me from under her lashes.

"Tillie?" I smile softly, leaning down to kiss her knee as I hold her gaze.

"Can we try something? I... I don't know if I can go through with it, but I need to try. I can't have this memory in my head, tarnished by Cruz forever. I want to feel good, and you said you'd make love to me." She looks away and takes a deep breath, as if trying to gather her courage.

"You can ask me for anything. We can try whatever you want and stop immediately if we need to," I reassure her, wondering what she's going to ask for.

When her gaze returns to me, she pushes me back and sits up. She crawls on her knees in the middle of the bed before grabbing my biceps to steady herself.

"Can you, um... Jesus. Can we try anal?" she quickly asks, her chest rising and falling rapidly.

It takes every single restraint in my muscles to not grab her and toss her around like a ragdoll, giving all the rough pleasure upon her sinful body.

Think, Dom. Don't mess this up, and for God's sake, control your dick.

"Yeah, we can do that, but only if you're sure," I say roughly after clearing my throat, stroking her arms up and down, feeling them tremble in my hands as her body shivers.

"I'm positive. I want the bad erased and replaced by all the good memories I make with you and the guys." She pleads with me to understand with her big, brown eyes and leans forward to kiss my chest, right over my pounding heart.

I grab her face as she pulls back and kiss her lips gently, slowly, until she's moaning into my mouth.

"You say stop and we stop, okay?" I release a deep breath, staring into her lust-filled yet wary gaze. She nods her head and grabs the hem of the shirt she wore to bed, pulling it over her head. Her long, brown hair trails over her shoulders until she shakes her head, and her full, sexy-as-hell breasts with tight, puckered nipples are exposed under my darkening gaze. Goose bumps pebble across her skin as I skim my index finger down her neck, past her collarbone, and drag it almost lazily back and forth on top of her breasts. "Do you know how beautiful you are? Every time I look at you, it feels as if you reached into my body and grasped my lungs, taking all my oxygen. You're fucking stunning, Mama, and I plan on telling you that every day." My voice comes out deep and gravelly, meaning every goddamn word.

"Make me feel you for days, Dom." She tips her head back with a whimper of pleasure as I leisurely stroke her breast, moving closer and closer to her nipple until the pad of my thumb rubs over her hard bud.

Without a word, I wrap my arm around her waist, arching her back as I lean down and roll her nipple with my tongue. This is heaven, and she tastes so fucking good that I could keep sucking and licking her for hours without growing tired. The noises coming out of her mouth are intoxicating to me, so sinfully delicious that I never want to stop. I'm already obsessed with her, and this is just making me feel more unhinged than I already am when it comes to her. I suck her breast into my mouth as much as I can, nipping at her silky skin while flicking her nipple with my tongue. Pulling back from her, she cries out in dismay, causing me to chuckle darkly and flip her around before she can say anything.

"Spread your legs for me and do as I say, okay?" I whisper in her ear, moving down because I can't help myself with her looking so tempting. My lips lock on her neck, nipping at her skin as I move her hair out of my way. She moans loudly and shifts on the bed until her legs are wide enough for my knees to fit between her parted thighs. I slide my hand around the back of her neck and sink my fingers up into her hair, grabbing tight. My other hand skims down her naked back until my palm presses on the flat of her spine, right above her ass. Her back arches as I tug her hair into my fist, placing a kiss on her lip before lowering her down until her head is on the mattress and her ass is up in the air. "Fuck," I rasp, my eyes on her bubbly ass, gliding down her smooth ass crack that's winking at me to take her.

I know this is a vulnerable position, not knowing what I'm going to do with her, but I'll do everything I can to prove to her that I'd never hurt her. She's safe in my care. I slide my hand away from her back, lowering until my fingertips graze her hole, watching it tighten at my light touch before I move on. My other hand clenches in her long hair, trying to control the rage that sweeps through my body. It's faint and small, but if you look at the tissue surrounding her asshole closely, you can see the scarring. That kind of scarring is placed there by force. I'm going to murder everyone in that fucking motorcycle club, even the ones that didn't touch her. Everyone is guilty for never stopping the pain she's had to go through. My gaze can't help but drag up to her left shoulder where the worst of her scarring is. The bumpy skin of *his* initials. I loosen my fist slightly as I notice how tense her body is, and when I look at her face turned sideways on the bedding, her eyes are closed.

"Mama, would you let me brand you here one day?" I try to keep my voice calming, but I know anger is seeping through.

Her eyes pop open as she twists her head to look at me over her shoulder. So much trust and yet there's fear in her brown gaze. It warms my chest, knowing she is placing her body in my care, even if she's scared of the unknown. This woman.

Fuck. She ruins me. She could destroy my whole world, and I'd let her with a smile on my face.

Mine.

"Brand?" she questions, her brows drawn together in confusion before understanding hits as my gaze narrows in on her shoulder. "Oh." That's all she says, her thighs trembling against mine as she stares at me with a look I can't fully read. "With what?" she asks finally, spreading her arms out in front of her, which only causes her lower back to arch more as she fists the comforter.

"I'm a possessive man, Tillie. I'd want my mark on your skin so everyone knows you're mine, but I want something meaningful to you also." I tell her the truth, and that makes me wonder if I'm no better than fucking Cruz.

"Would you let me mark you too?" Her voice comes out hesitant, her eyes glittering with unshed tears.

"I'd let you brand me a thousand times and wear it with pride so every fucker can see who I belong to." She breathes hard, her big, brown eyes dilating with lust at the thought of having her name forever marked on my skin.

"He's not the only one, little bitch. I know Tey has been

itching to tattoo your name somewhere on his body. I, for one, would be happy to have you tattoo Tillie leading down to my dick," Dalton drawls from the bedroom door, lifting his shirt as we look over at him leaning against the doorjamb.

I knew the asshole had been standing there for five minutes. It's not hard to see he has a thing for watching. He runs his hand over the hard lines of his pelvis with a shit-eating grin and gives Tillie a wink as she giggles.

"You're all crazy, but I think I would like that." She bites her lip, glancing out the corner of her eye as if she's gauging my mood about him being in here.

I had some time to think about it, and if she cares for them, I'll make sure each of these fuckers stays alive to keep her happy. It brings me some peace knowing that she has men that love her, protecting her when I'm not around.

"Have a seat, Dalton." I leave that order hanging in the air between us, noticing Tillie's breath growing heavy, and wet slick sliding down her thighs that also coats my own.

I can't look away from her, soaking in every moment of her naked in my arms, but I can hear Dalton walk across my room and pull the corner chair closer to the bed until he has the perfect view of Tillie's whole body from the side.

"Need some lube, my brother?" Dalton asks in a serious tone, and I quickly glance over at him with my brow raised to see he's not joking.

Looks like I'm not the only one accepting what we can't control. Him calling me brother is a step in a direction where I know Tillie is going to have five men at her beck and call.

"Top drawer." I nod my head towards the bedside table next to him and turn my attention back down to see my queen wriggling in her position, growing sensitive at having two men gazing at her every movement.

The lube lands next to me, but before I start coating my cock in the slippery lubricant, I want my girl ready. It's going to hurt at first. I'm not small, and it's going to be a tight fit pushing into her ass. Reaching above her shoulder, I grab two of my fluffy pillows and slide my hand under her lower belly.

"Lift those hips for me, Mama." I help her rise up slightly and lay both pillows on top of each other under her spread thighs. "Back down."

I slowly drag my hand out from under her, skimming along her soft skin before resting both of my hands on her hips.

"Why did you put the pillows—" She gasps as I rock her hips in my grip, back and forth on top of the pillows.

I know her clit is grazing against the soft material, causing friction until I'm making her hump the pillow. When I glance down between our bodies, a light pink mark shows on the white fabric, letting me know she's not bleeding too heavily. I don't care if she makes a mess all over my fucking bed. I'll buy a new set of sheets then.

"Feel good, baby?" Dalton asks her as she turns her head to watch him, the sound of his zipper lowering ringing loudly throughout the room.

"I need more," she whimpers, letting out a shaky breath.

Releasing her right hip, I reach down for the lube and pop the cap. The moment I pour it between her ass cheeks, she exhales loudly at the cold sensation as it slides down her crack and mixes with her glistening, wet pussy as she soaks the pillow. I take a moment to gaze at her now shiny ass, wondering how the fuck I got so lucky by ending up with this brave, amazing woman.

I don't know what the hell I've done in life to deserve Tillie wanting me, after doing so many bad things over the years, but I know when I see a good thing in front of me.

I'm not going to let her slip through my fucking fingers, and I'll die trying to keep her by my side.

Tillie

"I need more." Has my voice ever sounded so needy and breathless?

A deep hunger makes me suck in my stomach, my whole body quivering with the need to feel Dom moving inside of me.

I. Need. It.

"Shhh, little bitch. All in good time. Now be a good girl and present yourself for us." Dalton's voice is gravelly, the low demanding tones coming out of his mouth cause my pussy to fucking drip for him.

Literally dripping. The pillow is soaking wet between my thighs, rubbing against my slippery clit as Dom makes me hump the feathered pillows.

I keep my eyes on Dalton as he leans back in the chair, legs spread wide while he pumps his big cock up and down at an unhurried pace. He cocks an eyebrow when he sees me watching him, waiting for me to do as he says, and my whole body tightens in a small amount of fear yet so much lust, that I'm almost dizzy with it. Holding his stare, I slowly bring my arms behind my back and along the curves of my ass. Taking a deep breath, I grip each cheek and spread myself open until I feel the hot, burning gazes of them both looking at the most exposed part of my body. It's a strange feeling, being so vulnerable and open, but I know Dom is going to take good care of me. It goes without saying that, deep down, this man won't ever hurt me, physically or emotionally. Dalton too. He's going to watch my ass get fucked, but I know he'd put a stop to everything if it all became too much for me.

That's the thing about my crazy men, they push me to the limits that almost border on being too much, but they haven't gone so far that it's left me broken. Being forced to my knees for them almost empowers me. I can leave their legs shaking, brains a scrambled mess as pleasure consumes them, all while I might have a sore throat and tears in my eyes from my face being roughly fucked. It's a fucking strange world, but since I met them, I've learned my way, and I now know that women aren't only good for one thing. We hold just as much power as them.

"That's a gorgeous sight, Mama. Look at your hole, gaping open and then squeezing tightly closed, wanting to be filled and thoroughly fucked by my big cock," Dom whispers in a rough voice, the palm of his hand pressing flat against my back, right above my ass crack. I shudder, moaning as I watch Dalton spit into the palm of his hand, coating his cock with his saliva. Dom rubs at my lower back for a second, as if waiting for my body to relax before he moves his hand lower. He takes his time as he trails a single digit between the crack of my ass until he gets to my asshole, pausing there as he circles it, coating me with more lube. "Okay?" he asks softly just as he starts to put pressure around my puckered hole but stops before moving forward.

I didn't think I could love this man any more than I

already do, but that's a lie. Tears gather in my eyes at how gentle he's being and I furiously blink them away. I'm loving every minute, even though I'm slightly scared, but I don't want him to hold back, and I know he will if he sees my tears.

"Dom?" I whimper as Dalton clenches his jaw, his fist moving faster over his pulsing monster cock.

"Yes, Mama?" Dom rumbles in a seductive voice.

"Don't hold back. Please," I beg, needing him to be who he is.

Rough and violent. Demanding and controlling. Loving and gentle.

I need it all. Every single piece of who he is. I don't want him treating me with kid gloves, so this is me taking my power back. A piece of myself that was forcefully taken.

"I don't want to hurt you." He pauses his finger but leaves just the smallest pressure on my back entrance.

"I want you to hurt me. Fuck me hard but love me afterwards." I'm gasping, hips rocking back onto the pillow the more turned on I get, craving him to slide in and out of me.

"Fuck. Give her what she wants. She can take it." Dalton groans as if he's in pain at my words, biting his knuckle as he angles his head to stare at the way my hands are spreading my cheeks further apart for their gazes.

"You're killing me, Tillie. Give me a safe word. Now," Dom growls, his hand gripping my hips so hard that I know I'll have bruises after, but I love that.

I love knowing that he's marking me in a way I'll feel and see for days, knowing I belong to him and who gave me everything I asked for.

"Mrs. Sullivan." I smirk at Dalton as he stops pumping his hand up and down his cock to glare at me.

"Fucking hell. I'm never going to hear the end of that,"

he mutters before stroking his cock hard and fast like he's mad at it.

"Spread wider for us, Mama," Dom orders, humming in the back of his throat as I follow his order. "Good girl."

My pussy clenches at the praise, feeling really fucking empty.

He starts circling his finger around and around my hole at a slow, maddening pace, and I'm seconds from shoving back on his finger until he finally gives me what I want. The pressure feels tight at first, his finger only pushing in a little before sliding out just as slowly. On and on he teases me, taking his time coating the entrance of my ass with so much lube that I can hear his fingers making wet, squelching noises until he's finally knuckle-deep.

"Oh God," I pant into the comforter, my wide eyes locked on Dalton the whole time.

"Not God. Just your daddies." Dalton flashes me a wink and rubs the slit of his cock where pre cum is dripping out into his big hand.

"More?" Dom asks huskily, pushing his whole finger inside and circling my inner walls to coat it with as much lube as he can before he slides his digit out.

"Yes. Don't stop," I moan, arching my lower back higher and pushing back, desperate to feel his touch again.

"Greedy, Mama. Keep moving your hips back and forth, I want you trembling when I push into you." Dom groans behind me and three thick fingers start to push into my ass, stretching me until it burns and my eyes water at the sting.

"Look at you. You're so fucking beautiful, Tillie. You were made for us." Dalton's upper lip lifts into a snarl, pleasure darkening his purple eyes into dark storm clouds.

I can't talk, my throat tightening as emotions grip me.

This is trust. Handing yourself over into someone's hands who will take care of you and leave you whole at the end. I never thought this would feel good. I didn't know that my pussy would gush at ass play, but my God. I'm like a waterfall down there, soaking the sheets and Dom's thighs. It feels fucking incredible.

"More," I demand with a moan, pushing my ass back onto Dom's fingers as he plunges them past his knuckles, but he pauses. "No! Please. Don't stop." I'm begging, needy, and to the point of crying from how tight my body is with pent-up lust.

"Hard or slow?" Dom demands in a harsh tone, his voice deep with desire.

"Hard," I growl through my teeth, trying to move, but he holds my body still, no matter how much I shift around on my knees.

"That's our girl." Dalton grunts, twisting his wrist on the mushroom head of his cock and sliding his palm down the long length with a pained expression.

He's already close to coming, but he's holding back for me.

"Remember your safe word," Dom threatens, his voice so deep that my legs quiver, leaving me wanting to feel his lips talking into my pussy.

I cry out when he quickly plunges his fingers in and out at a rapid pace that has me rocking my hips back to meet each thrust. My clit almost hurts because it's so sensitive as it rubs back and forth on the pillow, my pussy lips getting the same treatment. I'm close to coming as my legs start to shake and my moans fill the room. But, all of a sudden, Dom stops and pulls his fingers out, leaving me a mess on the sheets as tears roll down my cheeks.

"No! Don't stop. Damn it, Papi," I plead, my voice so desperate and raspy that I hardly recognize myself.

"Don't move and keep holding yourself open for me." Dom's voice is like silk, a deep purr with his smooth Spanish accent that makes my heart race.

Dalton stops stroking himself for a second, as if he's mesmerized at whatever Dom is doing behind me, but I don't have to guess much longer when I feel the blunt head of his thick cock at my entrance. I stop humping the pillows and my breathing comes to a halt as a thick, dark cloud of disturbing memories tries to creep into this moment, wanting to ruin this for me.

"Say you're mine and only mine!" Cruz grunts into my ear from behind me as he tears through my virgin ass, panting like an animal in heat with each thrust that makes me feel like I'm being fried alive from the inside.

I remain quiet, tears and snot dripping down my face to splash on the cold cement below me. I won't give him the words, won't give him what he wants because that's one thing he can't take from me.

My voice is my own. He can torture me for hours, days, weeks, months, and years... but I'll never be his.

"That's how it's going to be? Anyone who looks at you will know exactly who you belong to," Cruz snides in my ear before pulling back and the slick click of his knife opening causes my whole body to tense up.

Blinding pain. Carving. Long, deep drags of the knife into my flesh.

Marked.

Owned.

Never free.

"Little bitch, open your eyes and look at me!" The deep

rumble of Dalton's voice drags me out of my past and into the present, his eyes a hard, passionate purple that won't let me go. I don't even remember closing my eyes, but I must have at some point as the bad thoughts drifted through my mind. He holds my stare and leans in close, softly sliding his thumb back and forth over my parted lips. "What do you need?" My body relaxes into Dom's hold at the question as Dalton cups my cheek, forgetting about his throbbing cock altogether.

Fuck. I don't deserve them.

"This. Just keep doing that," I say to them both, sighing as I snuggle my cheek into Dalton's palm before nipping at his thumb that rests on my bottom lip.

"Take a deep breath for me, Mama, and slowly exhale. It's going to hurt, but I'll stop anytime you want. We'll take this slow," Dom promises, soothing all my worries away instantly. I inhale through my nose and wait for a split second as I feel the pressure on my asshole, the tip of Dom's big cock trying to slip through the first ring of muscles that keep clenching, as if trying to keep him out. I exhale loudly and feel my body relax with it, sinking deeper into the pillows under me. I grind a little bit, feeling a spark in my lower stomach again, so I grind harder while pushing back. The moment I do, Dom pushes in, his fat cock stretching my inner walls to the point of pain. It's a fucking tight squeeze. "Choking my cock, Tillie," Dom rasps out just as he slides out a little and pushes back in deeper, the stinging pain making my eyes water.

"His cock is hardly moving inside your ass, little bitch. You're strangling him." Dalton bites his plump lower lip and keeps looking at where Dom is slowly pumping in and out of me with shallow thrusts.

The moment I feel him bottom out, I let out a whimper. I'm stretched to the max, and there's a burning pain around where my ass clenches over and over again on his cock. Feeling my inner walls beginning to spasm around Dom's cock somehow makes my pussy gush more, pleasure hitting me just as he takes his time, sliding his dick out until only his tip is in.

"Want more?" Dom asks, his hands sliding down to move my hands away from my ass cheeks. He laces his fingers with mine and places them above my head until I'm grabbing the iron headboard with my fists.

"Y–yes." I struggle to answer through panting breaths, my thighs quivering as he palms my ass.

I gasp as Dom suddenly smacks my left ass cheek, then the right in rapid succession, switching back and forth until I'm a moaning, loud mess. At some point, I curl my tongue around Dalton's thumb and suck it into my mouth, hollowing my cheeks as if I'm sucking his cock.

"I can't decide what to look at more. Your pouty lips or your ass cheeks jiggling with each smack." Dalton groans, his gaze flickering up to mine when I slip his thumb out of my mouth.

"Would you rather be watching or filling my mouth?" I practically purr, my tone seductive to my own ear, feeling desire sweeping through my body so hotly, I'm surprised the mattress hasn't burst into flames.

Dom chuckles behind me and smacks my ass hard once more before smoothing his palm over the burning pain just as he plunges his cock inside me again with a swift snap of his hips. My loud gasp turns into a moan as the back of my thigh slaps against his, the pillows shifting under me as my hips rock forward from his thrust.

"Fill her mouth. She wants it, don't you, Mama?" Dom

grunts harshly as he slowly slides his cock out before quickly fucking into my ass with another hard thrust.

"Yes! I want your cock fucking my mouth. I want my spit to coat every inch of your big cock with strings of my saliva sliding down to your balls. I want you to make me gag, cry... make me a mess. Both of you. Please." My breath comes in heavy pants, each exhale followed by a cry of pleasure through parted lips.

"Tillie..." Dalton growls deeply in his throat, and to my astonishment, sits back in his chair, out of my reach. "I think I'll watch for now. I want you desperate and on your knees for my cock when I feed you every single inch."

My vision goes hazy, picturing my knees sore and bruised as Dalton throws his head back while I suck his cock down my throat. I see the garage floor of Logan's house, the guys surrounding me again, but this time, they don't stop. They ruin me in the best way, using me for their pleasure. I want that. I need it as if it's the only way I can survive.

"Oh, fuck! Please. Please," I chant over and over, my legs shaking so hard as I push back against Dom to take him deeper. "Harder, Papi. I won't break."

I hear the ragged breath Dom releases right before his grip on my hips tightens and he unleashes on my body without holding back. I scream into my arm, my eyes rolling back when the headboard bangs against the wall as he pounds into me so fast and hard.

Slap.

Slap.

Slap.

Between our bodies clapping loudly together and putting a hole in the wall, I clench so hard around his cock that he groans each time he slips out. My pussy feels empty but full at the same time because Dom is so thick, and my clit pulses from rubbing furiously against the pillows. Dalton's grunt has my eyes snapping open to see his fist moving faster and faster along his length, his face tight with tension as he starts to near his orgasm. I drag my gaze up to his eyes and find him already staring at me.

"Come," Dalton demands harshly with a lip curl, his wrist moving rapidly over his monster cock so that his hand is practically a blur.

My body obeys, desperate to give in to his command that it takes me by surprise. Dom grunts and swears under his breath just as I start to come. His pumping hips piston so fast into me, losing control, and the first splash of cum hitting my inner walls makes me cry out loudly. Legs shaking, my whole body trembles as I squirt all over the pillows and bed covering. Each gush makes me whimper, my pussy hot, filling me with an intense bliss that I never want to stop.

"Fuuuuck!" Dalton shouts out roughly, and his cum shoots up in thick, white ropes all over his pumping fist and exposed abs.

The sight will forever be imprinted in my brain with the snarl Dom lets out as he fills my ass with his cum.

"Beautiful," Dom mutters behind me, breathing heavily.

He skims his hand along my sweat-slicked spine and sweeps my hair over my shoulder as he leans down to kiss the middle of my back.

"I think you broke me," I mumble out of breath, slowly loosening my grip on the iron headboard and collapsing into the mattress with a groan.

My body still trembles, parted thighs wet as Dom's cum slides down between my weak legs in a sticky mess.

"I'll take care of you. Shower and breakfast?" Dom slips away and sits up on the side of the bed, holding a hand out to me.

I glance at Dalton with a raised brow and he shakes his head with a smile.

"If I follow you into the shower, you won't be able to walk for a week. I'm going to head downstairs and talk to the guys. They should be here by now, and I have to let them know you weren't getting murdered up here with how loud you were being." He winks and stands up before leaning over me to kiss my cheeks.

He zips his pants and pulls his shirt off to wipe away the cum on his abs before balling up the fabric to throw at Dom's feet. He strides out the door like he owns the place, whistling happily under his breath.

"Cocky fucker," Dom grumbles with a sigh before standing and stretching. I can't take my eyes off of him as his broad shoulder muscles shift. Fuck, I want to scratch my nails down his back. He really does have a powerful, beautiful body. "Penny for your thoughts?" he asks huskily, and I glance up to see him staring at me over his shoulder.

"You're beautiful too." I slowly get off the bed and approach him, sliding my arms around his waist from behind with a happy sigh.

"I see I've fucked you delirious, but fear not, Mama. I'll wash you and feed you until you feel better." He chuckles as I try to pinch his incredibly hard abs, but my fingers can't grab anything because he doesn't have an ounce of fat on him.

"Dom." I pause and kiss his back before stepping away as he turns towards me. "Thank you. That... It was... everything to me," I croak out, clearing my throat as emotions grip me.

"Tillie. I live by this lifestyle where I could die any moment, be ripped away with regrets if I didn't step up and put my actions into words. The moment I saw you, I fucking knew. You're it for me. It may seem fast, but I love you. It's that simple."

My heart skips a beat with each word coming out of his mouth and then starts pounding that I think I might pass out.

"I love you too," I whisper and slam into him so hard that he rocks back on his heels as I squeeze him tight, resting my head over his pounding heartbeat.

"I know," he cockily says and scoops me up into his arms suddenly, walking towards the open doorway that leads into the master bathroom. "Relax for now and then we'll go face Logan together. Okay?" He raises a dark eyebrow, noticing the gloomy look spreading over my face.

"I really want to hate him, but I just can't." I bite my lower lip, dreading facing him, but I'm going to have to at some point, and I'd rather it be with the rest of the guys by my side.

"Say the word. I have a bullet with his name carved into it just for him." Dom grins down at me and sets me on my feet by the shower as he turns on the water.

"You can't kill him. Unfortunately, it would upset me." I scrunch my face and love his carefree laughter, his eyes crinkling at the corners.

Maybe all will be alright and no blood will have to be spilled... maybe.

***

Dom walks me through his hallways, pointing out rooms as we pass by while he plays with the ends of my wet hair, twirling it around his fingers. Warm, rich brown floors and light tan walls give his house a welcoming and relaxing feel to it. The windows are open, showing lush lawns and bright colors of dahlia flowers scattered everywhere. I'm amazed as he points through an open doorway towards his office with a mahogany desk and bookshelves lining the walls. A pool table can be seen through another doorway with a bar and big, brown leather chairs. We pass more guest bedrooms before walking into an open-plan living room that brings in natural light. I could picture myself curled up in the big sectional and staring out into the gardens through the French doors.

As we step through a handcrafted archway, more warm tones that wrap around a kitchen with a huge island come into view. Pots and pans with steaming food litter the counter while light brown bricks and skylights make me want to pull up a chair and watch his *Yaya* master the kitchen with years of practice. It smells so good in here that my mouth waters. That is until my gaze moves away from her humming around the kitchen and settles on a pair of sharp, honey-colored eyes that are boring into mine. I'm suddenly not hungry and would rather be anywhere else than looking into Logan's gaze.

"I'm right here." Dom places a kiss on my temple and walks over to his *Yaya*, popping a kiss on her cheek before heading over to the sink to wash his hands to help.

"Cuppy cupcake! I fucking missed your sweet lips!" Tey barrels into me, somehow crossing the kitchen at a rapid pace and lifting me off my feet to twirl us around in a circle that breaks my stare down with Logan.

"Language!" Isabella scolds Tey, and I can't help but chuckle as he puts me back down and looks sheepish.

Remind me to never mess with Dom's *Yaya*. That woman is a force of nature if she can make my crazy Tey behave.

"Pet, sounds like you had an...interesting morning."

Nicky's voice comes from behind me, his tone almost sounding bored, but a hint of amusement slips through.

Slowly pulling out of Tey's tight embrace, I turn to face Nicky and cross my arms in annoyance. I'm pissed at him. Okay, I'm more than pissed. I'm fucking hurt. The one person who I expect to give it to me straight and hold nothing back lied to me. Maybe lying isn't the right word, but he held shit back from me and didn't tell me about the club and Paris.

"Jealous?" I ask, unable to help the snide remark coming out while my face shifts into a hurt expression before I mask it, just like the cold expression adorning his features.

"Extremely," he replies in a deadly serious tone. It's his only fucking reply and he walks around me without another word, his hand lightly brushing mine.

I'm pretty sure my jaw is on the floor. The audacity of these men. He doesn't even offer an apology or excuse for what the hell he was doing at the club with Paris. I have a feeling Nicky wouldn't have wanted to be at the club unless he was forced. He hates Paris. You can just tell by the way he ignores her whenever she's around. It's another thing I need to figure out, why the secrets? Why go behind my back? Was I not worth telling?

"Give it time. There's always more to the story, remember? Nicky is... not one to share his pent-up feelings so well," Tey whispers softly into my ear from behind and steers me closer to the kitchen island with a hand on my hip.

I don't want to go near Logan because I have a strong urge to beat up his pretty face, but I need to get this over with. It's now or never.

I refuse to continue to have this pain in my chest. I want to close the door and never look back. That's my new motto.

Leave the past where it belongs... in the past. They say to learn from history, and I'm hoping I'm wrong about Logan and Nicky. I don't know what I'll do if they really did betray me. Just the thought of it fucking hurts.

I rub my aching chest and take a deep breath, trying to remember that in all this madness things do not always seem to be as they appear. Get down to the roots of the story, then kick ass if need be.

I meet Logan's gaze hesitantly and lift my chin up high. Like fuck will I look weak in his eyes. I'll make sure he can see just how strong I am, even if I'm dying inside. His intense eyes shine with approval as I stride over to him with my back straight, making sure he can't see my trembling hands by clenching them at my sides.

"It's not what it seems." That's the first thing out of his mouth the moment I stand in front of him, noticing how his voice carries in the kitchen.

Everyone is pretending to be doing something else when I glance around, acting like they aren't listening, but each of them aren't as sneaky as they appear. Tey is leaning against the counter, peering into each pot on the stove until Isabella shoos him away. Dalton is rocking back and forth on his heels as he stares out the French glass doors, but he keeps looking over his shoulder. Dom is chopping up some vegetables but isn't even paying attention to the knife in his hand as he stares at us like he's getting ready to jump in at any second if I need him. The only person not pretending is Nicky as he stands a few paces beside Logan, his arms crossed over his chest. I guess he's not talking, letting Logan explain for them both.

"Really? Then you didn't go out with Paris? It wasn't you and Nicky in that journalist photo? Was Paris mistaken as I smashed her face in?" I question sarcastically, crossing my arms under my chest and cocking a hip.

Dalton whistles like he knows Logan is digging himself into a deeper hole. I glance over at Nicky and am almost shocked at the look of approval in his gaze.

"Anything else?" Nicky asks, the corner of his mouth twitching like he wants to laugh.

"Anything else? Are you serious right now? You both go behind my back and fuck Paris? You know what, if you can't take this seriously then fuck you both." I keep my voice calm even though I'm seething inside. I quickly glance at Isabella, who meets my stare with sad, knowing eyes. "I'm sorry, Isabella. If you'll excuse me," I say tightly and spin on my heels as I quickly walk out of the kitchen, looking for an escape so I can cry by myself.

"Tillie," Logan is only a few steps behind me, his voice dark and filled with anger.

I turn to confront his smug-ass and yelp as I suddenly find myself hanging upside down over his shoulder. I brace myself against his lower back, blowing my hair out of my face, and meet Nicky's stare as he strolls behind us with his hands in his pants pockets.

"What have I told you before? I'm going to smack your ass and slap all the brattiness out," Nicky informs me, pulling out his hands to unbutton his sleeve cuffs and rolling them up to his elbows as if he's about to get his hands dirty.

I gasp, feeling light-headed all of a sudden. Though that could be from hanging upside down or having instant lust shooting through my body at the thought of him spanking me. I could lie to myself, but I really want him to spank me again. To feel the air rush over my exposed skin, the waiting game before his palm makes contact with my ass. The sting of pain, but the hot pleasure that follows right after... I hate my treacherous body for wanting things it should be against, especially Nicky and Logan. Fuck. If anything, these two should be bending over while I strap up and punish their asses. I have no idea where that thought came from, but I like it.

Kill me now, please.

Logan strides through an open door, and heat instantly blasts over my skin, the humid air smelling like chlorine. He deposits me on a sunbathing chair, not even out of breath, as if I weigh nothing, and starts to pace in front of me. I chance a look around and can only shake my head in astonishment as I stare at crystal clear blue water, floor-to-ceiling windows that are tinted, and lounge chairs lined up along the side of an indoor pool. Dom has an indoor swimming pool that's big enough to hold the Olympics. Am I surprised? Yeah, but I shouldn't be. These guys have so much money they probably blow their noses with the extra cash in their wallets.

"You aren't going to move from this spot until you listen to every word we have to say," Logan commands sternly, coming to a stop in front of me with his strong arms crossed and his biceps straining against the white sleeves of his shirt.

"Like hell I am! Fuc—" My shout is cut off as Nicky slips his tie in between my parted lips and ties it behind my head with quick, skilled fingers before I know what's happening.

"I think she'll be quiet now. Won't you, pet?" Nicky leans forward and kisses my exposed lips around the makeshift gag, ignoring the frustrated noise I make.

He smirks as I try to headbutt him, but he dodges out of the way and sinks into the lounge chair behind me, wrapping his legs around my waist, and trapping me so I can't move. He has my arms pinned by my sides with his thighs so I can't even attempt to remove the gag.

"I think I like this look on you, baby girl. We'll revisit this later." Logan rubs his bottom lip with his thumb as he looms over me, his eyes filled with heat.

I hate how lust curls in my stomach at that look.

"I ate yoth." I rage behind the gag, my words coming out as a jumbled mess.

"I love you too," Logan coos and chuckles darkly as I struggle in Nicky's grip. "Listen up, baby girl. Listen to every word coming out of my mouth."

I glare up at him and stop fighting as he towers over me like the freaking devil with possessive energy radiating off him in waves.

"Good." He grunts and looks away for a second, as if he's trying to find the right words before glancing back at me. "Yes, we did go to the club with Paris. She cuddled her body right up to us, touching our skin, and we let her."

I'm so mad and betrayed that my whole body trembles and my eyes water with unshed tears.

"But it was all for show, Tillie. You think I enjoyed her touch? I hated every single second of her stroking my arm and hanging off me like I was hers. Nicky didn't even try to pretend he wanted to be there. We only had one job that night." Logan pauses, his lips tight when he notices the tear that slides down my cheek.

"I almost killed her for touching my knee," Nicky admits from behind me, his voice strained.

I shake my head, not understanding what they're trying to tell me.

Logan reaches forward and catches the tear before it slides off my chin.

"So beautiful. Even when you cry," he whispers in

wonder and sits back on his heels. I release a shaky breath through my nose and sag into Nicky's body as the fight drains out of me. "Tillie..." Logan sounds tired and serious, his expression turning hard. "We're bad men, make no mistake about that, but I promised you that I'd never intentionally hurt you. I'd protect you with my last dying breath."

My heart pounds, hating and loving him at the same time. I haven't even heard why he was with Paris and still, I want him. Love is painful. It's not always loving. It's filled with hate, grief, and rage, but at the end of the day, the heart still beats for the one it wants. Or in my case... someones.

"Our fathers..." Nicky starts and clears his throat, as if it's a struggle talking. "We grew up being told there isn't such a thing as love. It's a weakness. It destroys you. As you get beat every day, talked down to, it changes you inside so that you lock every emotion down until you feel nothing." Nicky's breath fans across the back of my neck, his heart pounding in sync with mine.

Logan's face is pained as he gazes over my shoulder and I can't even imagine what Nicky's looks like. I think it was easier admitting that because he wasn't looking at me. I can understand that. Sometimes emotions we aren't used to are too much to handle and we don't know what to do with ourselves. My heart breaks for them. All of them have been dealt this fucked up life, but I don't feel pity. I know how they feel, life is unfair.

"Franco and Jin see you as our weakness. Do you know what that means?" Logan asks, bowing his head when I shake mine slowly. "It means that you're an obstacle in their way, and they mean to remove you." He glances back up and takes in my expression, my eyes filling with more tears again.

I hate this for us. Why can't we just be?! Their fathers

want to kill me and probably dump me at the bottom of the ocean.

"We did what we had to. I knew the journalist was going to be there because she likes to follow Logan around like a hound with a bone. We only took one photo on social media and she was there with her camera in hand. Jin has already seen the photo she took of Paris and us." Nicky sighs behind me like he's tired.

My mind races as I absorb this information. I know what they did was with the best intentions, but did they kiss her? Fuck her? I don't even want to know, but it's something I need to hear, no matter how much I don't want to.

"It was just for the picture. Nothing else. The moment I saw Ella enter the club, I knew we got what we wanted. We didn't fuck Paris." Logan stares deeply into my eyes with such conviction and sincerity, but a part of me is still feeling hurt.

"Do you believe us?" Nicky asks quietly, and I swear he stops breathing as he presses firmly against my back.

I probably shouldn't but I do believe them. I'd do anything to protect each of my guys. Anything. I might be forgiving easily, but my mind races as I think of ways to punish them for keeping things behind my back. Teach them both a lesson to never lie to me again.

I relax my body completely against Nicky, staring at Logan as I nod my head. Both of them let out a relieved exhale, and Logan strokes his hand up and down my thigh like he can't help but put his hands on me.

I expect them to let me go, untie the gag, but no. They don't do either of that. When am I going to learn that they always do the unexpected?

Nicky slides farther back in the lounge chair and his spread legs end up on either side with his feet planted on the ground. I squeak behind the gag as Logan yanks me forward into his chest, his big body straddling the end of the lounger. I struggle, quickly catching myself with my hands on his thighs. I look up in surprise and notice the glimmer of desire in his gaze, my own body tightening in lust.

"Arch your back, pet. Did you think I forgot about what you did to my car? My stick shift smells like both of you." Nicky's tone is sinister, deliciously seductive, and I know he's talking about mine and Tey's cum on the gearshift in his car.

My thighs try to close as I feel Logan start to drag my yoga pants over my ass. He counters my move, his big hands stopping me and spreading me wide open. He lifts me like it's nothing as he positions me how he wants with my face in his lap and my ass in Nicky's face. It makes me hot and achy at the strength he displays.

"I think she needs a beating on this juicy ass so she can't sit for a week." Logan exchanges a wicked smile with Nicky over my shoulder, and I try not to wiggle my hips when the humid air licks over my exposed, naked ass, wanting their hands on me.

"Brat," Nicky mutters, groaning lightly as he rubs the palms of his hands up and down my already red ass. "What were you up to this morning, Tillie? Your skin is flushed a pretty blush color. Did Dom spank you?"

My breathing becomes heavy. I'm practically panting and can't look away from Logan's face. His eyes darken to a shade of brown instead of his usual honeyed gaze. He's turned on by this power play, his breathing is just as rapid as mine.

"Did he fuck these lips?" Logan asks, skimming his thumb back and forth over my bottom lip, smearing the drool escaping from the gag until my mouth is wet and glossy.

I shake my head slowly, eyes widening as I feel Nicky's fingers traveling lower between my spread legs, petting my pussy with his skilled fingers in three quick strokes. I drop my head back, moaning hoarsely as he spreads the wetness leaking out of my pussy all over my lips and clit. Logan tilts my chin with his index finger so I'm looking up at his face, where he can see every emotion that overcomes me.

"Yes or no?" He holds my stare as I shake my head from side to side.

He sucks in a sharp breath, his thumb and index finger gripping my chin as my eyes flutter when Nicky drags his fingers around my entrance, continuing until he's circling my asshole. He spreads my wetness around and around, torturing me as my legs start to shake.

"Right here, pet?" Nicky purrs, his voice so intense that it vibrates in my bones and leaves me squirming in his hold.

"Hmm," I mumble around the gag, my back arching more until he can see all of me from my glistening pussy to my asshole—that's still sore and probably red from earlier.

"Naughty, pet. You're going to take ten smacks on the ass. One, for fucking in my car without me, and..." Nicky trails off and Logan picks right up from where he left off.

"And for letting Dom fuck your ass without sharing with the rest of us." Logan winks and chuckles deeply at my expression, my eyes wide as my body trembles with desire.

My fingernails dig into Logan's thick, strong thighs when the first slap comes without warning on my left ass cheek, making me cry out around the gag. My cries are muffled, sounding tortuous and deliciously taboo. The smack against my ass echoes around the pool room, loud with each spanking.

"One," Nicky says, his tone hard and deep that it's almost

hard to understand, but I know he's just as turned on as I am.

His thighs are tight with restrained tension on either side of mine, his hand rubbing over the sore spot he smacked with a gentle touch. It's completely different from when he slaps my butt; hard and unyielding, then soothing, as if to ground me and heal the part of me that throbs from his touch.

I expected him to smack my right butt cheek next, but he surprises me, slapping back down on the burning left one that makes my eyes sting.

"Two." Logan takes over counting for Nicky, his focus completely on me, hyperaware of every emotion that plays on my face from the grimace of pain that turns into pleasure as my nostrils flare with the next smack. My eyes are wide and locked on his, even when I want to close them from the feelings sweeping through my body. "Whatever you just did, she liked that. Do it again," Logan demands, his chest rapidly moving up and down as he watches.

I moan around the gag as Nicky slaps me on my right thigh, really fucking close to my dripping wet pussy. He has to feel the slickness coating my thighs when he hits them with the palm of his hand, feeling them quivering under his touch. I zone out, moaning and grunting as my body is shoved forward with each smack, but I push back, silently asking for more. I'm beginning to wonder if I can come from this alone. My whole body is tight, shaking, and I'm so close to slipping over the edge as my pussy flutters around nothing.

"Eight. This is your punishment, Tillie," Nicky mutters darkly, his tone seeping with thick desire. I scream around the gag as he smacks my pussy, gripping me and grinding his fingers over my clit. Logan leans forward and slams his mouth over mine, his teeth grabbing hold of my bottom lip and biting down hard enough that it stings for a second. He draws blood but quickly laps it up, stroking his tongue along the small cut until I'm moaning with my eyes rolling into the back of my head. "Ten." Nicky is panting heavily behind me, his breath sawing in and out like he's been running for miles.

I know it's coming but I still tense and wait with my breath held as his hand smacks my pussy again, slapping my lips so hard that I can hear the squelch of my wetness. My body spasms, shaking so hard as I come, gushing onto his hand as he furiously rubs my clit. My scream of pleasure is muffled by the gag and Logan's lips sliding over mine as he cups my face in his big hands. My vision is blurry and my hearing is muffled. I slowly come to as Nicky rubs my ass cheeks with soothing strokes before he leans forward, the lounge chair creaking as he kisses my butt. Pulling away, he slips my yoga pants back up and starts to untie his makeshift gag from my mouth as Logan helps me sit up.

What are these guys doing to me?! I never want to let go of this feeling, and I don't care if that makes me greedy. Good thing I have five men to keep giving me the attention I've always craved and to keep me satisfied.

"Baby girl, say it," Logan commands with that authoritative tone that makes me want to smack him and kiss him at the same time.

"Your slut," I say with an exhale, sinking back into Nicky's arms like liquid jello.

Logan grins and leans down, kissing me until I'm breathless and panting again before he pulls back a fraction, his lips barely skimming mine.

"Forgive me," he whispers, sounding desperate and broken.

My heart shatters, wanting everything from him but knowing it's not going to be easy. I'm at war with myself, too choked up that I can only nod and meet him halfway to kiss him again so he can't see the determined expression on my face.

I can forgive, but not without teaching them both that actions have consequences.

CHAPTER 8

Nicky

"Come on, I have a surprise for you," I gruffly say, rearranging my hard as fuck cock in my pants as I grab Tillie's hips and lift her out of the lounge chair.

Tillie's gaze goes down until her eyes latch on the front of my pants where my dick is straining to break free and shove into her perfect as fuck pussy. A smirk slowly spreads across her mouth. She bites her lush bottom lip and raises her dark chocolate eyes towards mine with a wicked glint.

Fuck. I love when she looks up at me with those doe eyes that are so expressive.

"What surprise? I'm going to be honest, I don't know if I can take another spanking. My ass is so sore, it freaking burns." She grimaces, rubbing her hands over her butt cheeks with a pout that makes me want to spank her again.

"Stop being a brat and come on." I send her a mocking glare, trying so hard to hide my expression... my feelings, but I'm so tired of it.

For once, I'd like to be able to let go and just fucking breathe without having to wear a mask on my face all the time. Tillie brings out the good in me. Don't get me wrong, I'm still a bad guy, that won't ever change, but I can still treat her like someone who is precious to me—because she is. I don't want to be unfeeling like my father. He's a disgusting human being that only cares about himself. I always thought I would have to hide every emotion, every expression. It was supposed to be a weakness if you showed even an ounce of love. Tillie and Tey... they bring out these feelings that I'm not going to contain anymore.

Fuck Jin.

I'll kill him before he can hurt the ones I love. No more hiding. I'm bringing the fight to him when he least expects it. Kill or be killed. It's time.

Logan walks ahead of us and Tillie raises a brow at me in question, but she shakes her head when she notices my lips are sealed. Tillie walks over to Logan as he waits for her, throwing his arm over her shoulder. He glances down at her with a small smile, looking happy, like really happy for once. My gaze shifts over to Tillie as she turns her head to look up at him, her expression a mix of contentment and a hint of sadness.

Like I said, it's hard for her to hide her feelings. Logan frowns, his brow furrowed as she smiles slightly at him. She says she forgives us, but I don't think it's that easy or simple. We have to earn her trust so I'll step up and be the man she needs.

I follow behind them as they exit the pool room, heading back in the direction we came from, towards the sounds of the guys talking and Isabella scolding them. I like Dom's grandmother, she doesn't take any shit from anyone. With four huge, strange men standing in her kitchen, she still manages to stare down at us, even though she's short.

The moment we step through the kitchen archway, Nicola comes barreling at Tillie with a warrior's battle cry that's more like a shriek and tackles her into a hug.

"Oh. My. Gosh! Babe! You are a freaking boss! Big titties, little waist!" Nicola shouts at the end as she draws away from Tillie, rubbing her shoulder against the side of her cheek with her tick.

I'm very protective of my little sister. I'd kill for her, and protect her, no matter what. I've always stepped in whenever some asshole makes fun of her just because she has Tourettes. It's not every second that she has her Tourettes, it comes and goes randomly, depending on her emotions. She's so strong and I'm fucking proud of her every day. It's just part of who she is. People can be cruel, but she stands up for herself and that makes me proud. I'll always have her back, even when she thinks I can be unfeeling, showing signs that I really am Jin's son. I think another reason I'm in love with Tillie is because of how she doesn't care, she treats my sister like any other person. She doesn't see her as being different.

I need to find a way to show Tillie that I love her. I'm a man of few words, so I'm not sure how to use my words when they matter the most.

"Real hot girl shit!" Tillie laughs, her face lighting up with joy. "Girl! You were listening to Megan Thee Stallion without me? That's a song meant to be sung together by besties. I'm really glad you're here, I have a lot to tell you."

"So I've heard." Nicola glares at me over Tillie's shoulder, like she's planning my murder. "Nicky, I'm so pissed at you—Pauly want a cracker?—that I'm going to kick your ass." Her expression is a mixture of pissed off and disappointed.

"I know. I give you permission," I reply in a choked voice, hating how I've let down my little sister.

Nicola stares at me in shock at my admission, and I let my mask slip a little so she can see my regret. She blinks slowly at me, her lip curling at the corner as she makes a ticking sound like a car engine turning over.

"Where's Evan?" Tillie questions, heading over to Tey to sit down in his lap without hesitation as he opens his arms for her.

I used to feel a burning sensation in my chest when they were together like this, but now all I feel is contentment, like this is it for me. My real family. A place where I feel at peace. I like seeing Tey nuzzling into her neck with a happy sigh as he stares at me across the kitchen. His crystal blue gaze always ensnares me with burning heat and a look of obsession. It gets me hot and really fucking bothered, and doesn't take much for him to get my cock painfully hard. With one glance, my cock is pushing against my slack zipper, begging to be let out to slap across his face. I think I'm going to be walking around the rest of my life with a semi-hard cock with Tey and Tillie always in my thoughts.

"Right here. You okay, Tillie?" Evan says from next to Isabella as she hands him plates to set the big family table that looks like it could hold twenty people.

"I'm okay. It's so good to see you guys," Tillie gushes, beaming at Evan as he goes over to her and hands her a plate.

He keeps his distance, making sure his hands don't touch hers... Smart man. Tey eyes him like a predator, close to snapping his teeth at him if he gets too close, and I keep my eyes on him as Nicola moves over to his side, leaning against his arm. Evan gulps so loudly that I can hear him across the kitchen as I stare coldly at him. He would be dead for dating my sister, but I've only ever seen him treating her nice, so he'll live, for now.

"Stop glaring in the corner and take a seat." Isabella

chuckles at me and waves her spoon towards the dining chairs.

I'm not about to argue with her, she's a force to be reckoned with. Dom helps by carrying dishes to the table with Dalton. Logan sits on the other side of Tillie and Tey like he can't be too far from her, as if she'll leave his sight and change her mind about him.

I don't blame him. I have that worry too.

Everyone gathers around the table, pulling out chairs and passing around dishes. I sit on the other side of Tey, stretching my arm along the back of his chair as I lean back in mine, relaxed for once in my life.

Strange that it's in Dom's house, but I'm beginning to realize that he's not the bad guy Jin has made him out to be. He's not my enemy but an ally.

The only thing you can hear is the scraping of forks against the china plates Isabella pulled out. You can almost feel the tension in the air, like everyone is avoiding the elephant in the room. I pick at my eggs, my appetite gone because of the discussion coming. I lazily run my fingertip back and forth on the back of Tey's neck, feeling him shiver before shifting Tillie on his lap so she can feel his cock straining in his pants.

"So, what's the game plan?" Dalton laces his fingers behind his head, crossing his ankles as he leans back in his seat. "Since no one's talking about it, I'll go first. I don't want Tillie going to the auction. We all know it's a trap."

He's not wrong, but it could be a lot worse for us if we don't show.

"If we don't show up, we'll get taken out one by one when we're alone. Jin isn't going to try anything at the auction, like kill us off. Important people are going to be there, especially ones that are going to help Franco get into office," I say casually while grinding my teeth, only to roll my eyes when Dom takes out the gun from his belt loop and starts to take it apart.

"I'm going to run some errands. Lovely to meet you all," Dom's grandma announces, excusing herself when we start talking business. "Be safe," she warns, and then she's gone, out the back French doors.

"Kill us off!" Evan shouts, his fork clinking against his plate as he drops it.

I think he's in shock, but he better suck it up. At least he looks protective of my sister as he wraps his arm around her waist and edges his body on the chair like he's going to bolt for the door with her.

"You good, kid? Who do you think the fuck we are? Did you think those rumors around school were a lie?" Logan scoffs, staring at Evan with a scowl.

"Well... no. I just didn't expect to talk about killing over breakfast," he mutters, letting out an exhale as Nicola whispers something in his ear.

"If you're with her then you're in. No backing out. What happens in murder club, stays in murder club." Tey stares Evan down without blinking until you can hear an audible gulp in reply.

"Be nice. Evan, no one is making you do anything. We can save this talk for later," Tillie encourages, narrowing her eyes at Logan, as if daring him to say something.

He scowls but stays quiet. He'll live to see another day.

"I'm all for murdering the cocksuckers!" Nicola claps her hands cheerfully, practically bouncing in her seat.

"Don't say cocksuckers or cock," I grumble, hating that word coming out of my little sister's mouth.

"Cock," Nicola mocks and then just smiles innocently as I glare at her.

"Okay. Enough cock talk. I want all the documents you can get your hands on of your father's business. Both of them," Dom says, tapping his finger on the table as he stares at me and then at Logan.

"Franco does all his business on his work computer at the precinct. I'll have to get it from there." Logan scrubs a hand down his face and turns to face me. "I'm going to need your help."

"Of course. I've already looked at Jin's computer at home, but I think he's a bit old school. My best guess is all the paperwork for every dirty business he's done is at the warehouse. I can look tomorrow night while you guys distract," I muse to myself, lost in thought, thinking about all the rooms with locked doors in the warehouse.

"I'll have your back. You so need me." Tey leans around Tillie and lays a smacking, loud kiss on my cheek.

I wipe my hand over the wet spot on my cheek and stare into his eyes as I stick my fingers into my mouth, sucking off the small taste of him. His eyes turn a darker blue as he watches me pull my fingers from my mouth. His desire-filled gaze drops to my glistening digits with barely there controlled hunger. I glance at Tillie in his lap and notice her eyes on my lips with the same expression as Tey's.

Shit.

I'm two seconds away from saying fuck it and grabbing the two of them to tie up so I can have fun with their bodies, edge them over and over until one of them breaks. I won't stop until I see tears and hear begging spilling from their lips.

"Goddamn. Will you three stop it? This sexual tension is turning me the fuck on." Dalton's voice comes out gravelly, and when I look over at him, he's on the edge of his seat, biting his fist.

Dirty fucker loves a good show, and maybe I'll let him in on some playtime, but not the first time with Tey and Tillie. No, the first they're all mine.

"Right?! Someone's getting lucky tonight." My annoying little sister makes a gesture with her fingers, mimicking sex, and I'm seconds away from reaching across the table and strangling her.

"Focus," Logan snaps and turns his attention to Dom. "What do you hope to do with the information we find?"

I'm curious about this too. I'd rather burn down the whole warehouse with Jin inside it.

"I want to expose Franco and Jin, let the world see them for who they are. If someone happens to die in the process, so be it." Dom shrugs like it's no big deal letting them live, but I notice his fists clenching on the surface of the table.

"Going after the Chief of Police. Cool, cool, cool," Evan mutters, sweeping his hand through his hair like he's stressed.

"He needs to be taken down before he gets into a political office. Dead or alive. Preferably dead," Logan growls through gritted teeth.

Tillie lays her hand on his thigh and like magic, Logan's body relaxes somewhat at her simple touch. Is it really that simple though? I glance around the table and see a bunch of messed up criminals that have all seen some fucked up shit in our lives, yet this one woman can bring us to our knees.

That thought does scare me sometimes when I think about it. She has so much power over us and doesn't even realize it. Maybe that's why I stuck around, even when I thought killing her would save us all the trouble she would bring to our doors. She's the glue that holds us together, a piece we didn't even realize was missing until she stared up at me with tears streaking down her cheeks as I fed her my cock.

"Tomorrow, we show our faces, get the information, and then get the fuck out. I don't want us there any longer than we have to be, Mama," Dom says to Tillie, his harsh features smoothing out as he looks at her with love.

"I'm going to have to dance, aren't I?" At my nod, she groans and stands up from Tey's lap to pace around the kitchen.

Tey pouts at the loss of her ass sitting snuggly over his dick. Can't say I blame him.

"Nicola." I wait for my sister to stop cuddling against Evan and to glance at me before continuing. "Did you bring what I asked?"

"What do you take me for, brother? Of course I did. Basically brought my whole closet." Nicola huffs like I'm an idiot, and in her eyes, I probably am.

"Noooo," Tillie whines, crossing her arms as she stares at us all with a grimace.

"Yes," Logan replies, his face set in stone like he dares her to argue.

"Fuck my life. Fine. Let's get this fashion show over with," Tillie grumbles under her breath and waits at the archway of the kitchen for Nicola to follow her.

Once they're out of earshot, I glance at Evan with my scariest glare.

"If anything happens to me, get Nicola out of this state. You hear me?" I don't break eye contact, letting him see I'm completely serious.

"I'd protect her with my life," Evan declares, sitting up straighter, and I have to admire how he doesn't glance away first.

I'll let him live for dating my sister, as long as he doesn't break her heart. Then all bets are off.

"I don't like this," Dalton speaks up, staring off into the distance with tight lips.

"None of us do, but we'll protect Tillie at all costs. She won't back down from this, you know it," Dom answers what we're all thinking.

At this point in her life, Tillie is done running from her nightmares. It's kill or be killed in her eyes.

CHAPTER 9

Tillie

"Which color do you like more? Red or—fucking!—black?" Nicola holds her hands out in front of her face, blowing on the two colors of nail polish then messes it up by flicking her fingers as she ticks her mouth sideways with a click of her tongue.

"Hmmm?" I say absentmindedly, staring at the chaos of clothes spread out on the bedspread. "Oh, uh, black." I pick up a scrappy piece of red fabric that would leave nothing to the imagination.

That's a no for me.

I know I'm supposed to dance for a bunch of old men tomorrow night, but the last thing I want to do is get them horny. Fucking sick, dirty bastards. My stomach twists in knots, knowing Cruz is going to be there watching me, always watching, like I'm his prey.

"Yeah, black looks good on you. You should wear the black dress. It's tight enough to entice but classy enough to not be slutty," Nicola comments with a clap of her hands, rummaging through the pile of clothes until she pulls out a black dress from the bottom. "Yes! It's perfect."

She hands it over and I hold it up, turning towards the

guest room's full-length mirror behind the door. It's slim fitting and has a velvet soft material that stops at the knees but it exposes the shoulders, showing off enough skin to make it sexy.

"I like it. It's too bad that human trafficking scum are the ones who're going to see me in this." I sigh and plop down on the bed next to Nicola with a groan, throwing my arm over my eyes.

"Imagine it's just you and the guys. Dance how you want to and then get the fuck out of there. I wish I could go with you, but my father..." she trails off, biting her lip as her eyes fills with guilt.

I sit up quickly, reaching out to her and squeezing when she places her palm in my hand.

"I'm glad you won't be there. You're my first friend and I don't want you in danger, around those monsters," I say softly and give her a reassuring smile as her brows furrow.

"Just don't let Nicky do anything stupid, okay? He really does care about you. I can tell." She squeezes my hand in return before releasing mine and flicks me on the nose, but I ignore it as a plan starts to form in my head.

"I think he does too, but it's hard to tell with him some-times. Anyway, I need you here. Do you want to hear my plan to torture Logan?" I start to laugh as she sits up straight and squeals with glee, getting up in my face with excitement.

"Fuck, yes! Tell me everything and I'll help any way I can." She automatically agrees without knowing anything about my revenge, and I couldn't love her any more than I already do.

"I'd like to know the same thing, Mama," Dom mutters from behind me, scaring the shit out of us and causing Nicola and I to jump at the same time.

I turn around on the bed and see him leaning against the doorjamb, a wide smile spreading across his lips.

"Jesus! Bitch!" Nicola shouts, flipping Dom off and blushing once she lowers her hands.

Not wanting her to feel bad about something she can't control, I flip Dom off for good measure and literally laugh out loud as I see the glint of warmth in his eyes, like I could do no wrong.

"So... I gotta admit, torture and Logan in the same sentence gets me really excited. Ask for anything and it's yours." Dom chuckles as he's pushed from behind, stumbling into the room as Tey runs past him and dives onto the bed.

He takes me down with him, making me shriek as he starts to blow raspberries on my neck and cheeks.

"Stop! You guys are going to make me sick with the cuteness overload." Nicola gags and scoots off the bed to go stand by Evan's side as he walks into the room.

"Pumpkin, you know torture gets me hard, it's like you're trying to make me walk around with blue balls. Don't tease me," Tey whispers between my neck and shoulder. I can feel his lips parting as he smiles before he starts to pull away and he licks his fucking long, pierced tongue up my cheek.

"Should we, uh, give you some privacy?" Evan stutters from the doorway, looking awkward as fuck as he looks everywhere except at us.

"You know, I like you, friend. You don't look at my queen with lust in your eyes," Dom says, slapping Evan on the shoulder as he walks by to stand at the end of the bed, almost knocking Evan off his feet.

"Right? I was just thinking I'll let him live since my baby likes him as a friend. I don't have to worry about him trying to hit on Tillie. I won't have to hide a body for once. You know how hard it is digging a grave? It takes hours and I get hangry. I usually have to stop for Taco Bell after being covered in dirt," Tey exclaims, exasperated like it's the end of the world having to go out of his way to get Taco Bell.

"I'll gut you if you touch my man," Nicola says darkly, and she really sounds like Nicky in that moment. The scary threats must run in the family.

"Will you stop! No killing Evan," I almost shout, glaring at Tey. Even when my lips twitch as he smiles innocently at me, I hold firm.

"Fine," Tey relents with a sigh and scoots along the bed with me in his arms until he's propped against the head-board with me cuddling against his chest.

"Thanks, Tillie," Evan chokes out, eyeing Dom and Tey warily as Nicola pets his arm with affection.

"Take a seat, guys. They won't do anything to you," I trail off, making sure both of my guys are sitting on either side of me, just in case I need to hold one of them back.

I don't think they'd kill one of my best friends, but I'm not sure about biting. You can't take the villain out of a guy, you just have to go with the flow and get on the crazy train with them.

"So, I'm practically bouncing in my seat here. What's this torture plan?" Dom grins as I turn my head towards him and I roll my eyes because he looks so happy at the thought of Logan's demise.

"Why? Do you want to help, Tey? He's your friend." I hold Tey's stare as he doesn't blink and let out a sigh when he doesn't answer, so I turn to my other man. "Dom, I'm not even going to bother asking you." I place a finger over Dom's lips just as they part, ready for him to be a smart-ass, but, Dom being the sexy man he is... he sucks my fingers into his warm mouth and gently bites down on my digit.

"Fuck, that's hot," Tey says in a hungry voice, and when I look upside down at him on his chest, his eyes are staring into mine with pure heat. "Stop distracting me with your sexiness. I love Logan like a brother, but no one hurts my girl." Tey's tone comes out serious, his chest rumbling against my back as he talks.

"That's surprisingly sweet of you, Tey-Tey. I approve of this relationship," Nicola chimes in at the end of the bed, giggling with me as I snuggle deeper into Tey's strong chest.

Fucking comfortable.

I sink into this strange comfort that I'm experiencing, and I'm not going to lie, I love it, and I want more so badly that it gets me choked up. Finally having someone that loves me is a strange feeling, like I'm finally whole. It's mind and body whole, a peaceful warmth that just makes so much sense. It's like staring at the sunrise for the first time, so in awe and stunned that you can't look away. It's beautiful. A new beginning that puts your whole past to shame and makes you realize you're actually living for the first time. I'll die restfully knowing that I found love, not just once but five times. Not many people can say that.

"Hey! I can be sweet when I want to be. Right, pudding?" Tey whines. He's actually whining so much that I can't take him seriously.

He has his moments but in a sweet, murdery way. Wouldn't have him any other way though.

"Anywho, I'm going to distract Logan. Let him think everything is fine for the day until I kidnap him when the sun goes down." I smile at Dom as he clutches at his chest, right over his heart.

"You ever try to leave me, I'll chase you down and tie you to me forever." Dom grins such a predatory smile, white teeth flashing, that I actually believe him.

"What do you need?" Nicola asks eagerly, leaning forward, her eyes sparkling with delight.

She's really just as bloodthirsty as her brother. I'm here for it.

"Duct tape, blindfold, somewhere remote that's sound-proof. I should be able to find the rest of what I need on hand. Nicola, I need you to do something extra for me that you might enjoy, it involves Paris. Oh! Evan, do you have something I can change my voice with? Star Wars maybe?" I smile wildly as Evan chokes and coughs while Nicola laughs and pounds on his back until he can breathe again.

"Fuck yeah! Count me in. Time to mess up that bitch's face." Nicola rubs her hands together in glee and bounces on her toes.

"I have just the thing. When do you need this all by?" Evan asks in a raspy voice, his eyes watering.

"Not tomorrow but the next day." I think about it but I'm startled as Tey picks me up suddenly by the waist and tosses me onto the bed next to Dom once he's standing.

I land with a thump, giggling, and Dom pushes my hair out of my face as he nuzzles my neck. I watch Tey quickly grab Evan and Nicola by their arms, pulling them off the bed and towards the bedroom door with his arms thrown over each of their shoulders.

"It's been fun but the grown-ups need some privacy. Get those things together and I'll text you with a location. Good chat. Byeeee." Tey ushers them out and slams the door in their stunned faces, their mouths gaping wide.

"I guess that's one way to get guests to leave," Dom drawls out against the spot between my neck and shoulder, nipping at the sensitive skin there.

"I needed them out of here before I came in my pants. You can't talk about kidnapping like that, sweetcheeks, without getting me fucking hard. Just look at what you did to me," Tey growls, palming the hard, big bulge in the front of his black jeans.

"Poor baby. Come here." I open my arms wide for him and he leaps onto the bed without hesitating, crawling towards me on hands and knees with a sexy smirk that gets my blood pumping.

"Careful. Our girl took a pounding earlier. How's your ass feeling, Mama? Sore?" Dom rumbles from behind me. I can hear the pleased, cocky tone in his voice as he squeezes me in his arms.

"You had anal without me?" Tey gasps so hard that I'm surprised he doesn't faint as he shoves his shoulders between my legs and settles his head on my stomach.

"It was everything, Tey. This is going to sound silly or cheesy, but I feel healed." I sigh, relaxing back into Dom's arms, and start running my hands through Tey's bright blond hair as he lifts my shirt to rub his scruff against my stomach.

"It's not silly, Mama. We all hold onto trauma differently and heal in our own ways. You need me to fuck you until you're healed, I'm here. You need ice cream and a sappy movie to cry, I'm here," Dom says in a serious tone into my ear, making my breath hitch.

"Fuck, man. You should write poems. That even made me tear up. What he said. You want to hold my unicorn?" Tey mutters against the soft skin of my stomach and shuffles around until he pulls his stuffed unicorn out of his front pocket.

These men. They're killing me. I don't think my heart can take it.

"I love you guys," I manage to choke out and gently grab

the stuffed animal, putting it between my shoulder and neck so it's cuddled up next to me.

"Love you, Tillie." Tey sighs heavily, sinking further into the bed like we're in our own little bubble.

"Love you," Dom rasps in Spanish, his voice low and sexy at the same time.

We lay there for a little bit in silence, the sound of our relaxed breathing fills the room. I play with Tey's hair and start to gently braid it so he doesn't notice. Dom strokes my arm up and down so slowly that I think he's drifting to sleep. I don't blame him, I'm tired as hell but my mind is still racing.

"Is it okay if I admit I'm scared shitless about tomorrow?" I break the silence, biting my lip hard so I can keep my breathing from going out of control.

"If you weren't scared, I would think there's something wrong with you. We all have our fears. I think you're fucking brave for facing yours," Tey mumbles sleepily into my stomach.

"You guys will be there the whole time? I don't think I can do this alone..." I admit, feeling my stomach drop to my ass at the thought of them not being there to have my back.

"Every step of the way, Mama. Don't worry, we aren't going anywhere," Dom promises in a hard voice, his accent thicker than usual.

I find comfort in that spoken promise, already knowing Dom won't break his word, and my gut tells me the rest of the guys won't leave me either. That reminds me about something.

"Where did everyone go?" I ask curiously, getting to the top part of Tey's hair and braiding it in even rows.

"Dalton went to scope out possible areas of escape near the warehouse with some of the Hell's Devils keeping him company just in case things go south. Nicky and Logan are heading to the precinct to see what they can find on Franco's computer there." Tey drops that bomb on me like it's no big deal and grunts as I suddenly sit up, shoving him off me.

"The hell?! Why didn't anyone tell me? They didn't say anything!" I panic, getting tangled up in the sheets as I try to scramble off the bed.

"Calm down, Mama. They know what they're doing. This isn't their first rodeo." Dom sits up on the edge of the bed and wraps me in his arms from behind, dragging me between his spread legs.

"I fucking know that, but I don't like it. I can help. I'm here and they're out there putting their lives on the line!" I realize I'm shouting and panting by the time I'm done ranting in Dom's face.

"You need to put your trust in us. We know what we're doing, and that's protecting you. At some point, one of us will be in danger, but we'll never be alone." Tey paces back and forth across Dom's guest room deep in thought.

He's about to turn around to pace back towards the door but whips around with his jaw dropping as he stares at himself in the full-length mirror in the corner of the room by the windows.

"Tillie, my dearest love, what did you do to my hair?" He chokes out a laugh, trying to run his hands through his hair but his fingers get stuck in the braided strands.

"I got bored and can't stop thinking about everything that's been happening. It's almost too much sometimes," I grumble, blushing as they stare at me, and I reach over to grab the unicorn from the sheets to fiddle with it in my hands.

"Feel free to do anything to me to get your mind off things." Tey cockily smirks, crossing his arms over his impressive chest, and clearly forgetting about the mess I made of his hair.

"Smooth, brother," Dom says with a grunt and doesn't notice when Tey turns his head towards him with clear shock on his face.

"Aren't I, *bro?*" Tey comes bouncing over to us by the bed and lays a wet, smacking kiss on Dom's cheek before backing away quickly, out of hitting distance.

Moments like this give me hope that everything's going to be okay. It's a little glimpse into what my future could be.

I'll fight for it.

Franco

"Forward the paperwork to my secretary and I'll get back to you. Good doing business with you, David, and thank you for sponsoring my campaign. Elections will be here before we know it," I grind out through a smile, hating how much I have to suck up to this ass, but his money will help me in the long run during the official race.

"Yes. Good. Good. Russo for 2021 has a nice ring to it. I'll have my secretary get in touch with yours," David mutters before a string of curses leaves his mouth, probably the secretary sucking him off, which is why he hangs up without saying anything else.

He owns companies and has connections to the right people that will open doors for me... It helps that he's addicted to the coke Jin puts on the street. Everyone will be in my pockets, and no one will be able to stop me. He doesn't even know I've been taking the missing shipments of guns and holding them until the time is right.

The elevator dings and I shove my cell into my pocket as I exit, walking into the main part of the huddle of desks where phones are ringing off the hook. Detectives and men in blue scatter around, shouting over each other, but somehow making it work like a well-oiled machine. It's how we function. Coffee, chaos, and more coffee.

"Chief."

I get mumbled responses as I pass by their desks, nodding my head without bothering to stop and say hi. This level of respect is well deserved, and if anyone tries to take it from me, they'll have to pry it out of my cold, dead hands.

Shannon isn't at her desk when I walk closer to my office, setting me in an already bad mood. For fuck's sake, can't she stay at her desk and do her job? I feel a kink in my neck, and maybe it's a good thing she's not typing on her fucking keyboard because I'd probably end up shooting it, or her.

I grasp my office door handle and am just about to turn the knob, but pause when I hear shuffling on the other side. Shannon knows better than to be in my office if the door is shut.

I don't hesitate, I whip open my office door, and the sound of it slamming against the wall bangs loudly around the precinct. To say I'm shocked to find Logan sitting in my desk chair is an understatement. Quickly taking in the scene, I notice Nicky sitting in the chair on the opposite side of my desk, flipping a small blade in the air and catching it over and over, looking bored with his fucking feet kicked up on my desk.

"Son, what are you doing here?" I plaster on a smile, looking behind me to see some of the detectives pretending to be busy on their computers, but they keep glancing up and quickly looking down when I meet their stares.

I step into my office and quietly shut the door behind me before spinning on my heels with displeasure. Striding towards my desk, I loom over Logan, which he ignores as he leans back in *my* chair with his hands behind his head. I scan the surface of my desk, looking for anything out of place, but nothing is amiss. I still don't trust it. I don't like seeing my son in my chair, looking too comfortable. He doesn't hold the power here. I do.

"I would have called but thought of stopping by instead. Can't a son see his father in his work environment? So proud of you, pops, and all the good you're doing," Logan drawls out, his eyes so much like my Helen's, staring up at me in judgment.

"Cut the shit. What do you want?" I grit out between my teeth. It takes everything in me not to whip off my belt and beat him until he loses that arrogance, but it's been years since I last hit him.

The moment he grew into his body, becoming just as tall and muscular as me, he started standing up for himself. I remember the day he stopped my belt from meeting the skin of his back so clearly. He had turned at the last second and caught the leather in the palm of his hand. I was astonished and somewhat proud, but deep inside, I was fearful. It was then I realized my son wasn't under my thumb anymore, and one day, I won't have any control at all left.

"Nicky," Logan calls out in an authoritative tone as he jumps to his feet, standing chest to chest with me for a second with a smirk before moving to the side so I can sit at my desk. The little shit paces around my office, touching my stuff, and finally stops near the door to face me, his arms crossed over his chest. Never turn your back to the enemy, I taught him that a long time ago.

I need to put him in his place before he thinks he can take my spot. He'll learn, and I think I'll teach him a lesson by playing with his little new obsession. Tillie's pussy tastes sweet and just ripe for the taking... again. Seeing the anger and agony that was on my son's face as I licked her pussy in front of him makes me almost laugh at the memory with delight.

"I'm sure you heard by now about the little accident with Carlos' gang?" Nicky says in a tone that is void of any emotion. I can never get a read on him.

That unnerves me.

"Of course, and I'm disappointed I had to hear about it from Jin before my own flesh and blood." I glare at Logan as he leans against the doorway, just blinking at me without saying anything.

"They'll be at the auction. I want to make sure you bring your own extra security. Never know when things might get a little messy." Nicky stands, buttoning his suit jacket as he turns, giving his back to me as if he doesn't see me as a threat when he's not looking.

"Unnecessary. I don't find Carlos' so-called gang to be a problem. I'm quite interested in meeting the new President of the Demon Jokers though." I smile when I see the tension go through Logan and Nicky's bodies.

I had a chat with Jin last night and found out that this *Cruz* is obsessed with Tillie, which gives me an advantage. Everyone has a weakness, and it makes them fools for caring for the girl. Whether it's love or obsession to possess, I don't give a fuck. It gives me an insight into how to hold my authority over them.

"I'm sure you two will have a lot in common," Logan growls out, insulting me by saying I'd have anything in common with a biker.

He'll pay for that later.

"While you're here, go to case number twenty-three in evidence. Switch out the drugs with shit that's not Jin's product." I dismiss them with that order, turning towards my computer.

They leave without another word, not even shutting the damn door behind them. I move the mouse on my desk, about to type in my password once the computer wakes up from sleep mode, but the home screen is already on display. My head whips towards the door, seeing Logan staring at me from across the precinct as the elevator doors shut.

What the fuck was he doing on my computer?!

I click through history but nothing shows up. That's concerning. I know Nicky can bypass anything and get rid of any evidence of ever being here.

Fuck!

A click of heels pulls my attention back towards my door and my teeth clash together when I see Diana walking right into my office like she owns the place. I skim my eyes up and down her form, growing angry at the skintight, red dress she's wearing. She walked into my place of employment dressed like a whore?

"What are you wearing?" I try to keep calm since the door is wide open and everyone in the hub can see in here.

No doubt some are eavesdropping too.

"You don't like it? I dressed just for you. I figured we could go out for lunch." She tries to smile seductively, but it does nothing for me.

Her smile falters when she notices I don't get up to greet her. Instead, I just stare at her with anger burning in my gaze.

"I don't have time for this. Go home, Diana. I'll see you later tonight." My mouth pinches at the corners when she doesn't immediately leave like I expected.

"Franco... we haven't made love since that night," Diana

whispers, wringing her hands and avoiding eye contact with me.

She's talking about the night Payne broke in. The night I ate her daughter's cunt out.

"Fuck's sake. I'll fuck you later tonight. Happy? Now leave." I gesture towards the door and hiss out each word so she will just fucking leave.

"No. I'm not happy. Don't you want me, Franco?" Diana whispers in a shaky breath, still not looking at me and staring out of the windows instead.

Pathetic and weak. What does she want from me? I put a roof over her head, food on her table, and throw money at her for whatever she wants to spend it on. I offer protection and she offers me a cunt to fuck. We're a happy couple for our public image.

"You could try to do some Kegels so your cunt is just as tight as your daughter's. Maybe work on that when you get home," I say harshly, watching her flinch at my words, but she finally fucking understands as she nods weakly and walks out of my office.

Blowing out a breath, I turn my attention back towards my computer and debate what to do about Logan. He's getting out of my control and I don't like it. Maybe tomorrow I'll have a little fun with Tillie in front of him again, but first, I need to do something that's currently driving me up the walls. Firing my absent secretary.

I storm towards the door and shout loud enough for everyone to hear.

"Anyone fucking seen Shannon?!"

CHAPTER 11

Tillie

I've never had sweaty palms before, but since I woke up this morning, I can't stop running my hands under cold water. It helps with calming the mind to focus on something icy cold, but now I'm in the car and only have my legs to keep running my palms on to wipe off the sweat.

"Just picture everyone naked. That should help, or maybe not. Never mind. Just picture me naked. That should keep you calm and horny." Tey gestures to himself before rubbing my thigh as it bounces up and down.

I'm really glad Tey and Logan are in the car with me. Dalton is riding with Nicky on their bikes, just in case they need to make a quick getaway. Dom is arriving fashionably late, his words, not mine. Franco and Jin aren't expecting their rival to show up uninvited, but they won't be able to do anything about it since too many important stiffs in suits will be their buying women. It makes me so sick to my stomach that I want to set the warehouse on fire, making sure every perverted fucker inside burns alive. I hope this plan works and a shoot-out doesn't happen the moment Dom makes an appearance.

"I shouldn't get horny in front of a bunch of perverts. I'll just picture slitting all their throats and choking to death in their own blood," I mutter, taking a deep breath as we roll up in Logan's car towards the marina, and the fishing warehouse that Jin owns comes into view.

"I don't know why I didn't think of that. See, you're perfect for us. My bloodthirsty killer, sexy woman." Tey turns my head towards him with the tip of his finger under my chin before stealing my fucking breath by kissing me fast and hot, curling his tongue against mine with slow flicks that have my thighs clenching together. He does that tongue curl when he's eating me out too. I can almost feel him between my legs each time he slants his mouth over mine with a slowness that drives me wild, and very fucking horny, like get-your-cock-in-me-right-now horny. I'm seconds away from demanding it, whipping his thick as hell dick out and riding it as if I'm at the rodeo and need to win first place. He pulls away with a groan, and a slow smirk takes over his pouty lips when he sees my dazed expression.

How do they do that? One passionate kiss and I'm a puddle on the seat, my panties soaking so much that I'm afraid it's going to seep through my black, leather bodysuit.

"Focus. We need to be alert at all times from the moment we step out of the car," Logan says grimly from the driver's seat as he spins the wheel, the tires crunching over the gravel parking lot.

The parking lot is covered in darkness and the warehouse looks abandoned with only a single light bulb over the entrance door. Looks are deceiving though. By the door is a man dressed all in black smoking a cigarette, a bodyguard I'm assuming, and I'm willing to bet there will be more patrolling the grounds. The whole lot is filled with fancy, expensive cars from Ferraris to Aston Martins and

Lamborghinis... The sick fucks have so much money that they think it's okay to buy another human.

"Can I admit that I'm very close to pissing my pants? And I'm not sure I could squeeze out of this thing." I wiggle in my seat in the back while Tey plays with the loose waves of my hair that are framing my face since the rest is being held up by two hair sticks that keep the bun tight to my head.

I feel exposed in this bodysuit. I thought the black dress would have worked but Nicola had an even better idea for something that wasn't easy access. The black leather is skintight and sleek, and clasps around my neck while leaving my whole back so open that I'm almost afraid to bend over in case my ass crack makes an appearance. I'm owning my scars and letting everyone see the drawings that scatter my body with pride, no more hiding from the world even if it makes me nervous.

"I'll cut you out of it if you're going to piss your pants. I got you." Tey skims his nose along my neck, breathing in deeply as he smells me before pulling away and flinging the car door open to get out.

I don't move at first, drying my sweaty palms on the slick leather of my pants once more and meeting Logan's gaze in the mirror when I notice he has not gotten out.

"I'm tempted to drive and keep going. I don't want you in there. You good, baby girl?" Logan asks in a worried tone, his voice low and so calm that it settles the nerves inside of me.

I need to be strong. Not just for myself anymore. It's for my guys and the helpless women about to be sold. This needs to end.

"I'm good, Lo. Let's just get this over with." I shake my

head, roll my shoulders, and grab Tey's extending hand to help me step out of the car.

I slide across the seat like butter, the leather making a squeaking sound against my bodysuit as I climb out. The rumble of Dalton's motorcycle is loud and shakes the ground underneath my feet as he parks right next to Logan's car. Nicky follows in after him, his crotch rocket making such a low rumbling sound that it hardly makes any noise at all. Nice.

We stand there for a second, as if preparing ourselves before turning towards the entrance and walking across the gravel lot. Each of my guys surrounds me, putting me in the middle of them as we get closer to the door. A hand tugs on my hand from the left and I look over my shoulder to see Nicky has stopped walking. He nods at the guys to keep walking without us while pulling me closer to him.

"What is it?" My brows furrow as he stares down at me for a second without saying anything before he reaches into his pocket and pulls it out with something fisted in his hand.

He raises his hand and opens his palm, a rose gold chain necklace dangling from his fingertips. The rose gold bird of a dove draws my eyes and I'm honestly frozen in place... It's beautiful and looks expensive.

"Can I put it on you?" he asks quietly, his green eyes undecided, like I'll throw the necklace in his face.

"You sure?" I ask warily, as if this is some kind of joke.

"Yes. Turn around." He rolls his eyes and spins his fingers in a circle when I don't turn around at first.

Turning, I watch the guys waiting a few feet away, giving us some privacy. They must have known he was going to give me the necklace. A little confused, I lift my hair as he slides his hands around my throat, gliding his fingers along the pounding vein there before moving the necklace into place to clasp it. For some reason, I'm light-headed as I stare down at the dove resting just above my breasts.

"Why?" I ask as I turn back towards Nicky, playing with the necklace between my fingers.

"Because." He clears his throat and looks above my head as a small blush rises in his sharp cheekbones.

Holy crap. Nicky is embarrassed.

"It's pretty." I grin softly, my eyes tracking how his Adam's apple bobs as he swallows thickly.

"No. Beautiful," he says in such a deep voice that it causes my legs to shake, and the way he finally meets my stare, I know he's not talking about the necklace.

"Thank you," I whisper, dropping the dove back against my skin and raising up on my tiptoes to kiss his cheek softly.

I press my lips against that spot for a few beats, breathing in his clean scent with my eyes closed. Pulling back, I spin on my heels and quickly walk back between the guys. No one says anything but I catch Tey grinning broadly at me and he winks when I make direct eye contact. The moment we stop outside the doorway, the bodyguard moves in front of us and places his hand on the gun that's resting in the front of his pants. My guys surround me closer than before but they don't react otherwise. It must be standard procedure to give everyone a silent warning by showing your gun. I don't fucking know but it still causes me to sweat.

We're really doing this. It's almost too much to process and yet, I can't freak out right now. I won't be able to ask for help if I start to lose it, everyone inside is going to be looking for an excuse to eat you alive if you show any weakness. I reach out and grip Dalton's bicep for balance as my breathing becomes heavy. I repeat over and over in my head that I won't have a panic attack. Once we pass that door, who knows what's going to happen on the other side. Dalton stays silent but lays his warm, big hand over mine with reassurance. He's here and I'm not alone.

"Tell me a happy moment," Dalton leans down and whispers in my ear in a gravelly voice.

A smile twitches at my lips, knowing he's trying to distract me like before when Gary and his stupid friends attacked me in the locker rooms and I ended up having a panic attack in Dalton's arms.

"Gary's house party," I reply back, stifling a giggle as he groans and pulls me under his arm to plaster my body against him.

"Fuck, little bitch. That's your happy moment? Which part?" he asks as we pass the bodyguard, grunting at him with a head nod as he lets us through the door once he recognizes Logan and Nicky. Not once does the fucker take his hand off his gun, letting us know he won't hesitate to use it on us. The bastard. I glare as we move past him, almost wanting him to even dare take his gun out so I can kick him in the nuts so hard he's singing soprano. He doesn't though and we're suddenly inside without any problems.

It goes dark once the door is slammed behind us, and lights on the floor leads the way that we're supposed to go. No one says anything for a bit as the guys huddle around me, Dalton squeezing me closer to his side which helps keep me warm. It's cold as hell here, and goose bumps break out across my skin, adding to the doom feeling that's pitting in my stomach.

"Hmm. Which part? That's a tough one. Maybe when you fucked me with the gun? Or when you shoved your big cock inside my tight pussy?" I lean into Dalton, trying to be quiet, but the guys groan as if in pain around me a second later though.

Guess I wasn't quiet enough. Oops.

"Not now, Tillie," Logan growls out through his teeth and I swear he whispers, *"Fucking hell."*

"Okay. Later then. I'll tell you guys about my knife fantasy." I try to joke to make myself feel better yet everything comes out strained and choked instead.

"Shh, baby cakes. Don't tell them, just me. I'll make all your knife fantasies come true." Tey chuckles darkly from the right, though his voice comes out tense.

The hallway comes to an end at another door, this one a solid metal with a small latch that opens the moment Nicky knocks on it.

"Nicholas, Logan, Dalton, Tey, and the slut," Nicky mutters in a bored tone. Despite his words, I notice his broad shoulders bunching up as he gives out our names and at what he just had to call me to the man on the other side of the door.

I probably wouldn't have been able to walk through that door if he gave out my real name. I'm just a woman that's a slut in Jin's eyes. My fists tremble at my sides, I quickly shake them to lose the tension because I know Nicky doesn't mean it. I'm their slut, but only when one of their cocks is inside of me. I know the difference.

I reach out in the dim lighting and graze my fingers against Nicky's lightly so he knows I don't blame him.

He brushes his fingers along my wrist before pulling away as the heavy door creaks open and the sound of muttering voices reach my ears. I ignore the meathead as I walk behind Tey with Dalton at my back, and I try to keep my expression blank while I take in the warehouse before me from the railings.

It's just as dark downstairs in the main part of the warehouse except an illuminated catwalk highlights a large black stage in the middle of the pit. The red couches are shadowed in the dark, and my guess is so that no one can see who else is here. Probably important people, the rich and famous.

"Whatever you see or hear, you can't react. It will end with a bullet in the head," Logan's voice is stiff, strained, like he hates being here as much as I already do.

"Trust us," Nicky says in his usual quiet, deep voice when I don't reply.

I'm really fucking trying, but I'm scared of what I'm about to witness. There isn't any music playing, it's just the low mutter of voices and the sound of shuffling feet behind the curtain at the beginning of the catwalk, leading to the dead center of the stage. It's fucking creepy that each woman walking down towards the stage is basically a piece of meat with a price tag.

"I'll do the best I can but make no promises. Just promise me that this will all end," I grit out. It's taking everything in me not to grab the gun tucked in Logan's pants and start shooting everyone below.

"It will end," Nicky claims passionately, and I believe him.

It's the burning inferno in his gaze when he looks over at me and his fists gripping the railing in front of him until his knuckles are white that tells me he wants this to end just as badly.

I nod at him and glance behind me when I hear Tey clearing his throat. He's looking off to the right with a murderous expression as he spins his knife between each finger. I follow his gaze and see Franco standing by the stairs that lead down into the seating area, and he's shaking hands with those that descend, like a fucking businessman welcoming everyone. He places something in their hands before moving on to the next person. Men and women dressed in their finest clothing smile at Franco, laughing at whatever he says to them.

"No reaction," Logan repeats one more time just as Franco spots us. His smile makes my stomach shift with nerves and sickness as he crooks a finger at us to join him.

It's the type of smile that reeks of something sinister, of evil thoughts. I'd love to wipe that look off his face, or better yet, grab Tey's knife and cut it off.

"Logan, you're late." That's the first thing out of Franco's mouth as we get close enough to him by the stairs without getting too close.

"Really? Could have sworn you said nine at night." Logan smirks, clearly enjoying pissing Franco off.

"It's ten," Franco hisses out, looking at Lo with disgust and displeasure before plastering on another smile as a man steps in line behind our group. "Get down there and don't embarrass me. Tillie, I believe Jin reserved a time for you to show off those impressive dancing skills around eleven." Franco's smile is slimy as he drags his gaze up and down my body with lust evident as clear as day.

At least Logan doesn't have Franco's eyes, he must take after his mother. Small miracles.

"Can hardly wait," I snap out behind my own tight smile, letting him see how much he disgusts me as my gaze locks on his. I grab Logan's hand just as he starts to take a threatening step towards Franco and direct him to the stairs, descending with him squeezing my fingers in a death grip. "So much for keeping your cool, huh?" I stand on my tippy-toes to whisper in his ear, gazing over his shoulder as I plaster myself to his side to make sure the rest of the guys are following.

It's creepy walking downstairs to a lower level, it feels

like a box you won't ever be able to escape. It's a small enclosed, square space that only has one entrance, meaning it only has one exit too. It's a fucking pit to keep things in, and those things would be human beings that are set to be sold.

"Don't leave our sight tonight. Stick close to one of us at all times. When Dom shows up, it's going to be a fucking massacre." Logan talks to me but he has this half smile on his lips that looks cocky and ignorant as he glances at the "guests" once we reach the last step and people openly stare our way.

If you look past the fake smile and stare into Logan's eyes long enough, you can see how hard and deadly his gaze is as he looks at everyone, almost like he's memorizing faces to kill later.

"Believe me, I'm not going anywhere," I reply, suppressing a shudder as he leads us around the fancy, red velvet couches and selects one giving us a viewpoint of the stage and the stairs, so we can see who's coming and going.

That eases me a tad because I know no one can sneak up behind us since there are concrete walls behind our couch. I glance around and my lip starts to curl in disgust at the walkway and stage, as if it's a fucking model catwalk, when in reality, it's just a perfect circle so you have a view from all angles of the human body that's going to be on display. The guys take a seat with Logan in the middle, and he pulls me down to sit on his lap as Nicky and Dalton sit on either side of him with Tey on Nicky's other side. All the guys' moods are pulsing in waves, brooding and silent. They hate this just as much as I do.

"Two o'clock, Tillie. No surprises," Dalton mutters in a gravelly voice, suppressing a throaty growl at whatever he's looking at.

I'm almost afraid to look. I could just keep staring at the stage but the goose bumps on the back of my neck won't go away and demands I scan my surroundings until it finds the source of the creepy feeling. I know who he's looking at before I even glance over.

Has the hair on your arms ever stood on end? Have you ever been scared of the dark because you feel like your worst fear is going to be right behind you, breathing down your neck?

That's how I'm feeling right now. Sweat slides down my back and my stomach sinks, as if I can't decide if I want to throw up or if my whole body is going to become cold and numb before shutting down. I gaze to where Dalton pointed out and my gaze immediately connects with Cruz. He's already staring at me and, I swear, my heart stops beating for a split second. That look scares me. Cruz's gaze holds so many emotions that aren't normal. Possession, like I'm an object, lust, as if he's thinking of all the sick things he wants to do to me against my will because he gets off on it, and rage. That rage is what scares me. It's not directed at me but at my guys as Cruz's gaze shifts towards them before settling back on me. It's a promise in his eyes that speaks of death.

"He'll never hurt you again, my sweetness. We'll paint a whole room with his blood then burn it down to ashes," Tey says maniacally, his tone so dark and seriously dangerous that it makes me shiver with a bit of fear and lust.

Dalton places his finger under my chin and makes me break eye contact with my worst nightmare. Violet eyes hold mine now, piercing into my soul until a faint smile spreads across Dalton's face as he traces my bottom lip with his thumb.

"Happy place, little bitch. Don't look at him again," he

says, taking an inhale that I mimic. I can breathe a little easier after I do it a few times.

I didn't even realize that my breathing had picked up and that I was on the verge of a panic attack.

"Fuck," I whisper, shifting closer against Logan to try and warm my exposed back whilst I try to keep my expression neutral, as if I'm bored, like the guys.

I don't want to be looked at like I'm weak, and I need to make sure no one can get a read on my emotions ever again. They're currently all over the place with dread, fear, panic, and a small area in my heart of pure love, but all these people here will only see the collected Tillie from now on.

"Here we go. Don't react," Nicky warns just as the lights dim and everything goes silent. The *guests* quiets down as the curtain at the end of the walkway parts, a spotlight shining brightly over the entry.

I hold my breath as the silhouette of a body edges inside and pauses in the light with a big, muscular male at the female's side. I'm confused at first by what I'm seeing, but hot rage quickly gathers right down to my soul as it clicks what's happening. I become rigid in Logan's lap and a hand snakes into mine, squeezing tightly as we watch the drugged-out girl get practically dragged down the walkway by one of Jin's men. She trips over her own feet, head rolling on her shoulder as the guy grips her elbows and stares straight ahead with a bored expression. She's skin and bones. The white, see-through dress shows just how starved she's been.

"They start with the least valuable, and towards the end, the best is saved for last, the ones who will bring a very high price," Nicky says from beside me with a tone that almost makes him sound like a robot, but when I look over at him, his fists are clenched on his thighs and his neck is straining with tension. I rub my thumb over the hand Dalton is holding and slowly reach over with my other hand to Nicky, sliding my pinky over his wrist.

Nicky's breath stutters out, like he's been holding it in. I make eye contact with Tey on his other side, seeing him press his thigh firmly against Nicky's. He's not alone in this, and I can't even begin to imagine what it was like for him having a father like Jin. Maybe we're more alike than I thought.

"Bidding starts at ten thousand," a voice says over the speakers, making me jump in Logan's lap. It sounded so loud when everyone was being so quiet, except for the once-in-a-while murmurs.

Logan's hand smooths across my lower back out of sight, sliding back and forth over my scarred skin. Maybe he needs the contact to keep him grounded because right now, I'm seconds away from grabbing his gun and shooting wildly, hoping I hit every fucker in here. I can't even imagine what he's feeling right now.

I glance around, seeing men in freaking butler suits with trays standing on the edge of each section of couches, far enough away to create privacy, but the moment someone raises their hand, the butler comes over instantly with that damn silver tray. I watch in bewilderment as a piece of paper is placed on the tray and the butler walks away, heading right for Franco. I didn't notice at first but he has a section all to himself, and Jin is on the right corner of the stage with his triad guards surrounding him. The butler hands Franco the folded paper, who reads it and signals to the man holding the girl up in the middle of the stage. The guard nods and starts dragging the girl back towards where they came from, the spotlight shutting off so we can't see them leave on the walkway.

"What..." I trail off, confused as fuck about what's happening.

"She was just sold. The guards at each section of guests get handed a bidding offer and delivers it to Franco and Jin. If accepted, the next person comes out to get sold," Logan explains in a choked, tight voice, his hand now gripping my hips so tightly that I know I'm going to have a bruise later, but I don't care.

My mind is racing and I've never felt so helpless. Not even when I was getting raped, beaten... This isn't about me though. These people getting sold are going to go through so much worse than I ever did, and I'm just sitting here doing nothing. Absolutely nothing.

"Stop. Don't do that to yourself. All this will end soon," Nicky whispers so quietly that I almost can't hear him, and I know he's not talking about the auction ending for the night. He's talking about Jin's death.

I can hardly wait. It's slightly easier to breathe, knowing the fucker is going to die.

Most people don't know or believe that human trafficking is a real thing that happens every day. Women, men... children. They get kidnapped and sold to the highest bidder, and never seen again. There are some very rare cases where that person is found, but after so long being in the hands of a monster, they become an empty shell; having to fight every day just to do normal things like brush your teeth without looking in the mirror because you're scared of what your reflection is going to show you. I have to sit here, feeling helpless, and contain my anger after each new person is brought out and sold. I'm trembling. I'm so blood-thirsty that my body is literally shaking to cause chaos and murder. My mouth fills with the taste of copper as I bite the inside of my gums to keep from crying. My fingers grasp both of my guys so tight that I'm sure by the time they pry my fingers off them, there will be bruises left behind.

Sometimes, someone will cry because they're upset, like angry or sad. To me, those two emotions go hand in hand. You can't be sad without anger. You can't have anger without sadness following. Like tears of love and happiness, it's all the same. Right now, I'm so fucking angry and sad that this is their life. I'm not even sure how long I've been sitting in Logan's lap, ridged like a statue. The guys don't make a sound or look away from the stage. If you look away, it's almost like you're ignoring what's happening right in front of you... In this case, ignorance is not bliss.

"Pure and innocent. A feisty piece of work that needs just the right owner, bidding starts at one hundred thousand." Jin's voice is suddenly speaking, loud and clear from the microphone.

He sounds fucking delighted and smug, like he has everyone eating out of the palm of his hand.

The spotlight turns on and the oxygen is sucked out of my lungs, along with Dalton as he curses under his breath. Logan's thighs tense under me and his heart races against my back. Nicky looks frozen solid next to us, his burning gaze directed right towards Jin with pure hatred in those green eyes. I'm suddenly gripping his hand that he probably doesn't have any blood flow left, but he doesn't push me away. He holds on just as tight. I shift my gaze over to Tey and worry he's about at his breaking point. He adores kids, and so this has to be killing him inside. He hasn't stopped spinning his knife between his fingers, and I don't think he's blinked at all. My gaze drifts back to the stage as the same goon from before drags a little girl down the walkway. She looks like she's maybe twelve. She fights the whole way, kicking and throwing her tiny fists anywhere to cause damage, but it's no use. She's shoved onto the center stage, falling to her knees with a cry. Looking up with terrified, wide eyes, they lock onto mine. I could be wrong, it's very dark in here, but in that moment, with her brown eyes looking so scared and lost... I know I can't do this.

That's a kid up there, someone's child. She shouldn't know the evils of the world yet, but here she is. She reminds me of, well, me. A girl who's facing the reality that this is really happening, that evil does exist, and that hope is dwindling away as the excited murmurs echoes around the pit.

I glance around to see card after card being thrown onto silver trays, and my gaze is drawn to Cruz, as if I can't help myself. I know what I'm going to see, and it's going to end up with me in a lot of trouble. It's like he was waiting for me to look, because the moment I make eye contact, he smiles slowly and sickly as he places a white card on a silver tray. A bid. I feel the blood drain from my face, my body going cold. If Cruz gets his hand on that child... No! That's not going to happen. He knows I'll do anything to stop him from getting her. It doesn't matter if Cruz is surrounded by Demon Jokers, along with Carlos and some of his men. Cruz alone has control and power to get whatever he wants. We're all just a sick game to him.

"Would anyone care for a demonstration? Who wants to see some obedience lessons?" Jin's smooth voice drips like poison as he announces over the speakers with a chuckle, and the crowd cheers in agreement.

My gaze swings over to Jin and Franco as they give the goon on stage a nod of approval. Big and muscular, Jin's bodyguard stands over the girl with a menacing grin as he bends down and roughly grasps her elbow until she's standing again. The first strike is across her face, and I'm shoving Dalton and Nicky's hands away from me. The second strike and I'm slipping out of Logan's lap before he can stop me. My mind is numb and racing with the thoughts of my past, of the obedience lessons Payne put me through for years. I'm pushing past bodyguards near the stage to get through, ignoring the guys calling my name. I'm laser-focused on the goon as he draws back his hand again, this time with a fist. I don't know how I managed to gain the strength to grasp the ledge of the stage and pull myself up within seconds. How did I get across the room so fast that I'm now standing in front of the girl and blocking the next hit for her?

My hands all too easily slid into my bun, releasing wavy lengths of hair and taking out the sharp, pointed hair sticks that were holding it securely. I see my hand raise, as if it's someone else's, as it slashes at the guard in front of me. I hear a vicious growl and realize it's me making those sounds, like a wild beast that was caught in a cage and is now suddenly free. One second the guard is leaning over me to throw a punch and the next, he's frozen, his mouth opening and closing as he stares down at me in astonishment. His neck starts to bleed from one side to the other, spurts of it coating my face as he falls to his knees and tries to stop the river of blood flowing down his neck. I glance down at my fisted hands and see the hair sticks coated in blood. I slit his throat and don't feel anything at all. I'm not even a little bit upset it happened.

He deserved it.

All at once, the noise of the crowd rushes into my ears and the hand of the child squeezes my arm in a death grip. I hear low murmurs, shocked gasps, and guns being cocked. I look down at the hand cutting off the blood flow to my arm and gaze at the little girl staring up at me with hope in her brown eyes.

I don't regret anything, even if I'm about to die. I'll go down fighting though, taking out as many of these sick fucks as I can. I hope they're ready for hell, as I'm about to send them there.

"My, my. It would seem someone is a little jealous of not getting all the attention. Nicholas, why don't you show our guests how to properly punish a disobedient whore." Jin's voice still sounds cheerful, but there's a hard edge to it that makes me flinch.

I'm gasping for air, sweat coating my neck, but I don't move from in front of the child as my gaze wildly swings around until it lands on Nicky. He hops onto the stage with ease, his muscles bunching under his suit jacket as he straightens the sleeves with a roll of his broad shoulders and strides towards me with purpose. His facial expression gives nothing away, but the moment I lock eyes with him... I know I'm in trouble. His green eyes narrow in anger, their color darkening as his pupils expand. The sharp edge of his jaw shifts, muscles ticking as he stops a few feet away from me and widens his stance, dominance pulsing in waves from him.

The little girl is suddenly pried away from me, my distraction costing me as another one of Jin's guys drags her away, back towards the entrance of the curtains. I'll get her out of here, I swear on my life I will. It's better this way for right now, at least everyone isn't looking at her anymore. All their attention is currently on me and Nicky as we stare at each other in the middle of the round part of the stage.

"On your knees, pet," Nicky orders softly but with so much command that my legs shake with the need to obey. I hold my stance even though my legs want to buckle under me as I stare at him with wide eyes, blood still dripping down my face and the dead goon at my feet behind me.

Nicky can't be serious. I already know where this is leading, but I don't think I can do this in front of so many strangers while they're looking on with sick lust and hunger in their eyes. It cramps my stomach, reminding me of my time in the basement when every member watched as they all took turns raping me."Eyes on me," Nicky growls out as my gaze shifts around to see *guests* watching, but his voice snaps my attention back towards him in an instant.

Tall, lean, but with defined muscles, Nicky commands attention with his eyes alone. They challenge me with the slight narrowing, willing me to do as he says... and God help me, I want to be on my knees for him. It's the aura that surrounds him, his dominance, and the tight control he has, it makes me want to break that leash he holds so close to his heart. I want wild and passionate Nicky to let go. I want the man that feels under all that armor he shows everyone else but me.

After a few seconds of staring down with him, I slowly sink to my knees and everything else fades away until it's just me and him on the stage. I drop the hair sticks with a gasp, feeling the fight drain out of me as they clatter onto the stage. My body bends to Nicky's will without much of a fight, and the sick, twisted side of me likes this. Needs it.

I rest my butt on the back of my heels, arms loose at my sides, but I tip my chin back so I don't break eye contact with that gaze of emerald green that's currently grounding me.

"Crawl to me," he whispers in a dark tone, but it sounds loud, even past the rushing of blood pounding in my ears. My hands graze the floor with slight hesitation, but laying my palms flat on the floor, and with a deep breath, I crawl across the stage towards him. Slow and seductive, my hips sway as I easily crawl towards him with warm blood coating my hands. My leather bodysuit becomes slippery in the blood on the floor, the warm blood soaking the material of my outfit as I stop at his feet. My chest rises and falls, faster and faster, while my body shivers with adrenaline and desire. "Show everyone how you present yourself to me. Who owns you, pet?" Nicky demands with a tight jaw, his lips curled into a snarl as raw desire has him clenching his fists at his sides.

I suppress a whimper, holding his gaze as I lean back on my heels again, arching my back with my knees spread wide for him. This position, if naked, would leave me exposed, nothing to the imagination. My head tilts back but I don't break his hold. I can't. If I look away then it's going to remind me it's not just me and him up here. Raising my bloody hands above my head, I slowly drag them seductively down my neck, between my breasts, until I'm gliding my palms over my knees back towards the floor. Leaving me back on my hands and knees at his feet, I bend down without him having to say anything until my forehead is grazing the tip of his shoe. My breath fogs the shine of his polished, expensive shoes, and I swear, I don't hear anything else but the small hiss he releases between his teeth. This position leaves my back arched, ass up, like a good submissive. Anyone with two eyes can tell right away that Nicky likes control. He's a Dom and always will be.

"Good, pet. Now, answer me. Who owns you?" he says louder, his voice deeper than ever with layers of unholy desire.

"You do," I whimper out with a pant, feeling my thighs squeeze together with need.

"Say my name," he growls out and bends down to pull me up by fisting my hair, making me meet his hot, dangerous gaze again.

"Nicholas," I rasp out, tears burning the corner of my eyes at the sharp sting as he tilts my head back farther.

Why do I love this? Why do I need to be dominated and praised? I used to be angry all the time, scared of what I would and wouldn't like, but all I feel now is a possessive need to be completely and truly owned by my guys.

If that's disturbing and wrong... I don't care. It's how I love them.

Tey

know I'm fucked in the head, that's never going to change, but even I know how wrong it is to get a hard dick at this moment. I'm so hard I could burst through my zipper. My cock is an endless, leaking stream of cum as I watch Nicky and Tillie up on the stage. I want to paint them both with my cum, spraying jet after jet onto Tillie's pure, scarred, beautiful skin, and watch Nicky's hard cock get coated in white as I cover him too. That's me marking my territory. I have no regrets for my twisted mind. I'm most definitely sure my unicorn would agree with me.

"What's that, Mr. Unicorn? Kill everyone here and have kinky sex in their blood afterwards?" I ask my stuffed animal, pulling him out of my pocket and up to my ear like he's talking to me. Dalton and Logan take their eyes off the stage and stare at me like I'm losing my mind. Kind of too late, but they still keep me around. I'd rather let my freak fly than keep it trapped inside like everyone else does. Freaking psychos. "I'm kidding. He didn't say that. You guys can live too, just everyone else here dies," I whisper out the side of my mouth to them and swing my gaze to Cruz. "He dies first. I can't decide if we should put him on a stick and have a slow roast, or slice off his skin, cook it like bacon, and feed it to him." The tone of my voice deepens and darkens as I think of all the ways I could kill him.

Wow. Even my own voice is scaring me. I've literally got goose bumps over here. I sound a tad crazy, a little bloodthirsty as usual, and sinister as fuck.

"Tey... I don't even know how to process that, but save those thoughts for later. We need to get them off that stage before Dom shows up." Logan is fuming, like I'm surprised his perfect hair isn't combusting into flames right now.

"I don't fucking like this. Fuck! Everyone is staring at them with rapt attention. She's drawing unwanted attention to herself," Dalton says in a voice so thick it sounds like he's chewing on gravel. He's right. As I glance around, everyone is staring at Tillie and Nicky. Hell, I keep getting distracted each time I look up at them putting on a show, but I need to focus. "She's goddamn beautiful up there though. She didn't hesitate cutting Jin's guard down, a clean swipe to the throat." Dalton's tone comes out smug and proud. I'm right there with him.

She's amazing. I just want to pick her up, put her in my pocket next to my unicorn, and take her everywhere with me.

I sigh, running a hand through my blond hair, messing it up even more. I'm so turned on that my cock could hammer a nail into a wall, but I'm also pissed off that everyone can see Tillie and Nicky like this.

They're mine! I should gouge out everyone's eyeballs before they die for looking at what's mine.

"Unzip my pants, pet," Nicky instructs Tillie, his voice deep and sexy as fuck. He can keep that blank expression, a show for everyone else, but I see the affection as he looks down at Tillie at his feet. That and the burning desire in his darkening green eyes. My breathing is ragged as Tillie places her hands on Nicky's legs and slowly slides her fingers over his pants, caressing his muscular thighs and stopping at his belt buckle. She's on her knees, her face level with his zipper, and I bet he can feel her panting breaths through his pants. She glides down his zipper with confident hands, staring up at him like it's just the two of them. "Take my cock out," Nicky whispers, his shoulders tight with tension and the muscle in his jaw ticking.

Oh yeah. He's fucking drowning in her, turned on even though he's trying to hide it from Jin.

"We have five minutes before Dom gets here," Dalton urges, his knuckles popping as he stares at the stage, deep in thought. He watches as Tillie licks her lips and curses under his breath.

"We don't have to do anything. Look at him." Logan crosses his arms, nodding his head to the other side of the stage.

I look and a grin starts to spread across my lips as Cruz's face is turning a deep purple, his eyes a vile blue with rage and jealousy. It just gets better as Tillie pulls out Nicky's cock and gasps with awe, like his cock holds all the answers she has ever needed. She's not wrong. Nicky's cock is long, curved, and has just the right amount of thickness. He could whip out his cock anytime, smack me with it, and I'd still ask for more. I'm always mesmerized by the tattoo of a forked tongue and fire that starts at the base of his cock, traveling all the way to the tip. That tattoo hurt, he was out for weeks, but it was worth it. I love how the dragon starts out on his rib cage in black ink, and the head's on his hip bones with an open mouth and razor-sharp teeth. It makes me shudder in delight. I'm going to lick it next time, take my time exploring his sinful body with my tongue.

"Lick," Nicky grinds out, his hands flexing at his sides, like he wants to grab her and make her swallow his whole cock in one thrust. Tillie pants over his dick, her wide, dilated eyes staring up at Nicky with lust glittering in her big, brown gaze. I grip my cock over my pants, squeezing it to ease the pressure as she sticks her tongue out between parted red lips and licks the enlarged tip. She moans loudly and eagerly swirls her long tongue around the large mushroom head again, gathering the drops of pre-crum with the tip of her tongue. A string of saliva and cum follows back into her mouth as she licks her red lips. "Good girl," Nicky breathes out. He can't help himself now as he shows a hint of emotion.

My gaze whips towards Jin and I see murder and disgust in his gaze as he looks at the stage. He says something to Franco, who nods with a smirk and then Jin brings the microphone to his mouth.

"Bidding starts at one million." Jin's voice echoes in the pit along with the shouting of *guests* as they start filling out the bidding papers and demanding the goons with silver trays hurry the fuck up so their bids make it back to Jin.

I start to take a step in Jin's direction but Logan catches my shoulder, stopping me.

"Showtime," he says, sounding amused as he turns his gaze towards Cruz, who is fighting Carlos as he tries to hold him back from reaching the stage.

"One minute. Get your masks out," Dalton gruffs out, pulling a skeleton mask out from the inside of his suit jacket.

Logan insisted we all wear black suits tonight that match. I'm currently wearing another thin jacket under my Armani jacket. It's for Tillie, along with the extra mask I have for her. If all goes according to plan, we should be able to get out of here unnoticed and save all the women being traded in the process without anyone knowing. We just have to wait for Dom to show up.

Nicky grasps Tillie's cheeks in the palm of his hands, his thumb stroking over her lush lips that are parted a breath away from his cock.

"Suck," he growls out, oblivious to everything else around him, and I don't blame him. I'd gladly die happy if the last thing I saw was Tillie's lips wrapped tight around my hard cock.

The bidding piles up on the trays and Jin and Franco seem pleased as the amount rises higher and higher.

"Ten million!" Jin declares through the speakers, and the *guests* lose their minds as they shout at an increased volume that makes it feel like I'm in the stock market.

I'm not even sure if he's auctioning off Tillie or Nicky, probably both. Selling his own son, his only male heir, tells me he doesn't give a shit. Jin can see what Nicky tries so hard to hide, and that's his feelings for those he cares about. That's a weakness in the triad leader's eyes.

"Get your hands off her!" Cruz screams bloody murder, his voice contorted with rage as he smacks his elbow back, knocking it into Carlos' nose. Blood spurts out as he howls in pain, letting go of Cruz, who makes it to the edge of the stage. He grips the platform and is about to jump up but the triad bodyguards stop him before he can get to Tillie. No one touches Jin's merchandise because that's how he sees Tillie, and I think Cruz is just now finding that out as he's shoved away by five guards. "Tillie! Don't you fucking put your lips on him! I own you, cunt!" Cruz yells up at the stage as he struggles between the guards, his face a deep red as Tillie stops inches from Nicky's cock and looks over at him with a sneer on her pretty face.

I'm so fucking proud of her as she levels a glare at Cruz and basically says *fuck you* as she turns back to Nicky, sliding her parted, wide lips around his cock with a long swallow until her nose is brushing his pelvic bone. That's my girl.

My grin widens when Cruz struggles harder against the guards with a roar of rage as he watches Tillie deep-throat Nicky. The smile slips off my face as he whips out a gun from his pants and shoots two of the guards. All hell breaks loose after that.

Screams pierce the air and hysterical shouts of chaos are all around. Just as I slip on the skeleton mask, bullets rain down from above near the stages.

"Dom's here," Logan says as he walks away and pulls out his gun, aiming for Cruz.

Cruz looks around frantically, shooting bullets towards the guards, and almost misses Logan with his gaze, but then Cruz whips his head back just as my brother strides towards him, his gun raised with a shot to kill. Dalton and I split up; I'm hunched down and running towards the stage. Nicky grabs Tillie, covering her with his body as bullets rain down from everywhere. I glance back at Logan and see him pull the trigger once he's close enough to Cruz. The fucker sees Logan approaching with the barrel of the gun pointing at his head, and at the last second, Cruz grabs Carlos, moving him in front of his body, using him as a human shield. I chuckle in delight at Carlos' surprised expression as the bullet sinks into his forehead. His body jerks back as Logan continues to shoot bullet after bullet into him. At least one problem is solved, Carlos is dead.

"Nicky!" I shout at the very edge of the stage and beckon him over as he looks up, relief heavy on his face.

He wraps an arm around Tillie's waist and drags her

over to me as I raise my arms up for her to hop down. Nicky slides her into my hands and glides off the stage as he zips up his pants, pulling his mask out next from his back pocket.

"Give her the mask now, we don't have much time," Nicky rasps, his chest heaving, probably from the show they put on and the bullets kicking up cement as they explode into the walls around our crouched forms.

"Shit. Where are Dalton and Logan?!" Tillie grabs my hand in a tight grip as I slip the mask over her face.

"Don't worry. Causing a distraction with Dom and his crew so we can get to those files." I kiss her wrist and let go, pulling off my jacket so I can cover her with it while zipping up the other one I had on underneath.

Now we all blend in and no one can tell who we are. Dom and his men are dressed the same, all wearing skeleton masks and their clothing all-black. It's kind of brilliant and is going to piss off Jin to no end since his auction is now ruined.

I grab Tillie's hand again and clasp my knife in my other hand, nodding my head for Nicky to follow, just as we take off in a light jog—since we're hunched over to avoid getting hit by a bullet. We make it towards the entrance of the curtains from the walkway and slip behind the fabric with my knife ready, just in case. I quickly shove Tillie back as a triad member slashes out in front of me with his own knife, barely missing my neck. I grin and attack with a quick lunge, cutting a fast, smooth swipe across his neck. Blood squirts out, hitting my face, and I can't help but think *payback's a bitch* as I laugh at the dead man at my feet.

"That's what you get. Tillie, my little killer, we match now!" I declare excitedly before pulling up my mask along with hers and rubbing our noses together with a content sigh.

This is heaven with hell at our backs.

It's perfect. She's perfect.

I love when she's covered in blood and it's even better when I'm coated in it too. I bet we would make the most beautiful art if our bodies were naked right now. Just her and me on a blank canvas painting it red.

"God, you're crazy," she says in a loving voice that warms my heart. She nips at my bottom lip before pulling away, her mask once again covering her face so no one recognizes her.

"You have a little something red right here." Nicky reaches over Tillie's shoulder, smearing the red lipstick she left behind across my bottom lip with his thumb.

"I'm pretty sure you have some on your cock too. Don't have time to whip out that big boy now, but later I'll be investigating to make sure it's there," I tell him with a wicked grin, pulling the mask over my face again. I chuckle darkly as his eyes burn into mine with desire.

"Let's get those papers and get the hell out of here." Tillie grabs both of our hands and raises a brow patiently at Nicky to lead the way.

"Right. This way." Nicky clears his throat and starts leading us down a hallway off to the right.

The moment we turn the corner, Nicky aims his gun and fires two times while his other arm pushes me and Tillie behind him up against the wall. Fuck, if that doesn't make my cold, dead heart pump rivers of blood. I love when he gets all protective, even though I'm very capable of taking care of myself. Nicky moves his hand away, placing it on my shoulder as I move to stand next to him in the doorway. A dead guard with a bullet in his forehead stares up at the ceiling, bleeding all over the place.

We stand in front of a room with screaming women and children huddled together, their eyes wide when they see three strangers wearing scary, skeleton masks. It's probably not the most fucked up thing they've seen though. Some stare back without any emotions; dead eyes but still breathing. It makes me really fucking sad. A deep sadness that a happy, normal life was ripped away from these people. Choices and freedom were taken from them.

"Tey, we can't leave them here." Tillie pants next to me, her breathing harsh with anger as she grasps my sleeve jacket in a death grip.

"We aren't. Dom brought enough men for backup, and Jin's a coward. He's probably already out of the building, leaving right when the shooting started. Dalton and Logan won't leave without getting everyone out. We have our own job to do, to stop this once and for all," Nicky says passionately, his gaze through the mask conflicted as he stares at the room full of broken people.

"I trust you," Tillie whispers, reaching out to Nicky and squeezing his hand.

It's hard to turn your back on something that tears at your fucking heart, the hope dimming in each terrified gaze that is directed at us.

"Stay here. Help is on the way. The men in skeleton masks are the good guys." I lie through my teeth because, let's face it, we aren't good men, but we're better than most of the fuckers that are selling people.

We continue down the hallway, my knife in hand swirling between my fingers and Nicky's gun out at the ready in case we run into more trouble. Tillie walks between us, her fingers looped in Nicky's belt to stay as close to him as she can while she holds my hand behind her. It's quiet as we reach the end of the hallway, where one lone door is propped open and a set of stairs leads up.

Nicky starts heading up the stairs on quiet feet, his gun raised on the open space up ahead. I'm a bit distracted by the muscles shifting under his jacket and Tillie's gorgeous ass in my face. I shake my head and force myself to focus, looking behind us to make sure no one's sneaking up behind us.

Reaching the landing, it's lightly lit and quiet, with office doors wide open except the one at the end of the hallway.

Jin's office.

"In and out," Nicky reminds us, his head whipping back and forth as we pass each office.

It's completely empty up here. I can't even hear the chaos from the pit, which kind of saddens me. I love chaos and mayhem. Nicky rattles the doorknob, finding it locked, which isn't a surprise. Tillie pushes him away when she notices him taking out his lock-picking gear and shoving us back with an eye roll.

"Watch and learn, boys." She smirks and suddenly kicks her right foot up, balancing on her left as she slams the heel of her foot right under the doorknob. It makes a splitting noise, the door bursting open with just one solid kick from her. I'm sure my jaw is on the floor because when I look at Nicky he meets my gaze with his eyes crinkled in the corners from smiling. He's just as impressed as I am. It takes a lot for Nicky to smile, and all it took was our girl road-housing Jin's office door. "Don't look so surprised. I did grow up in a motorcycle club, after all," she says dryly, her face souring at the reminder, and walks into Jin's office without a backward glance.

"Shit," Nicky mutters under his breath and follows after

her, heading towards the filing cabinet behind Jin's big, fancy, mahogany desk.

I hate that she grew up in a motorcycle club and all the pain she's had to suffer at Payne's and all the members' hands. It makes me feel murdery inside, and I can't wait until we take out the Demon Jokers. They will regret the day they hurt my angel. Every last one of them.

With a deep breath, I walk towards the wet bar and move bottles around until I find what I'm looking for. Carrying them to Jin's desk, I sweep his shit off the surface and start unscrewing all the scotch bottles. They're good fire starters, and that thought makes me happy, humming to myself as I watch Nicky pick the lock on the cabinet with ease. Seriously, who uses paper these days? Jin. The sick fuck.

"Start on that end, pet." Nicky points Tillie to the other side of the long cabinet and looks over his shoulder at me with a pointed gaze at the liquor bottles.

"I thought we could roast some smores." I smirk, taking my unicorn out of my pocket and grabbing my zippo out of the stuffed animal's butt.

"Jesus." Nicky shakes his head and returns back to digging through the files, but I see his shoulders shake with silent laughter.

Yeah, he totally loves me.

"You know, I don't think we're going to find what we're looking for here," Tillie announces after skimming the files for a few minutes. She sits back on her haunches with a thoughtful look before glancing around.

I admit I was thinking the same thing. I can't stop pacing and looking out the door because I feel like we're running out of time. I already have all the liquor bottles ready to go, and now I'm getting antsy.

Logan: *Building clear.*

My phone goes off with that text message and I know it's time to get the hell out of here. Dalton's probably already pouring gasoline everywhere in the pit and just needs a small fire up here to get things going. I watch Tillie crawl towards Jin's desk and disappear under it for a second until we can hear an audible click echo throughout the room. She pops her head up with a wink and climbs to her feet as her hand searches for something under the edge of the desk. Nicky and I crowd around her, looking over her shoulder as she pulls out a file and slaps it on the desk.

"Like all cocky men, they think the world can't touch them. I think Jin is about to realize that he's not above everyone else. He's just a man," Tillie mutters with a sniff and flicks through the file before her face scrunches up with pain.

She passes the folder over to Nicky and grabs a scotch bottle, taking a deep swig as she rolls her mask up before tipping the bottle all over on the floor while grabbing more liquor off the desk. She walks out of the office, hips swaying, leaving a trail of liquor behind her.

"Damn," Nicky hisses, watching Tillie with a look of admiration in his emerald eyes.

I'm right there with him. I grip the back of his neck, squeezing a second to ease the tension radiating from his body, and lean forward to bite the space between his neck and shoulder, loving the deep groan that leaves his mouth.

"Let's get the fuck out of here, Nicholas, before our girl decides to start the fire without us." I lick the spot my teeth sank into, leaving a mark, and swipe a scotch bottle off the desk to douse Jin's office until it smells like a dirty bar.

"It's time, Tey. No more holding back," Nicky says, taking

the drink out of my hand and tipping the bottle back towards his mouth.

I watch his Adam's apple bob, my throat dry as he looks at me over the rim with lust brimming in his eyes. I know exactly what he's talking about.

Holy mother of god.

An unleashed Nicky... Fuck. I'm not sure Tillie's sexy ass is going to survive the beating he's going to deliver, or if my cock is ever going to be the same again.

I watch his tight ass walk out, his strides long as he catches up to Tillie where she waits by the stairs. I back out of the room with a chuckle, my grin so big I'm surprised it doesn't split my lips at the corners. Flipping my zippo open, I watch the flame and throw it at Jin's desk.

"Burn, baby, burn."

CHAPTER 13

Tillie

My hands tighten around Nicky's waist as he leans to the side on his crotch rocket, taking the corner too fast. My body leans with him, as if we are one.

Me. Him. Us.

It's exhilarating and tastes of freedom, as if nothing can touch you when the world blurs around you. My mind keeps swirling, thinking of all the pain over the years, and we're going to have more tonight. I'm almost scared to show Logan the file that's going to break his heart. Everything he thought he knew was a lie. He's expecting it, but to be living proof, evidence finally right in your face... You can't run away from that. It almost makes me feel guilty about tomorrow, but if he can handle the torture I'm going to put him through, then nothing will ever break us apart.

I flex my fingers against Nicky's button-down, feeling his hard abs shift with each turn we take. The cold wind started biting into my fingers the moment we left the warehouse and the warmth of the building went up in flames. I hated leaving Logan, Dalton, and Dom to handle the rest, but they wanted me far away from that mess before the police showed up. Franco got out apparently and went to work at the precinct, probably rounding up all the cops that do his dirty work. I guess Franco will have to make an appearance for the press once it's discovered that bodies were found in the wreckage. They won't find any evidence of the human trafficking ring though. My guys saved those women and children. I don't know what will happen to them, how their lives will move on from here, but Nicky reassured me that they will be okay. Being a hacker comes in handy, especially when you can send a message to the Feds without any trace leading back to you. Apparently, my brooding, handsome Nicky has been doing that for years. I bet Jin's blowing a gasket, and Franco's having the press eating out of his hands right about now.

God. I hate that man. All his fake smiles and words of loyalty to your face are a joke.

I turn my head to the right, my helmet resting on Nicky's shoulder as I gaze at Tey riding Dalton's motorcycle with a carefree grin on his face and the wind whipping in his hair. Crazy fucker won't wear a helmet. He said I was cute for worrying about his safety. I'll always worry.

A few minutes later, we climb up the long driveway to Dom's house, once we get through security, one of the five garage doors opens upon our arrival. Looks like Dom really did add us to the list of people allowed to come and go from his home. The rumble of the bikes is loud as we pull in and the crank of the garage door shutting has the guys cutting off their engines. I breathe a sigh of relief as I shake out my hair the moment I take the helmet off and inhale deeply at the smell of gasoline. It's a smell I'm familiar with, and I have fond memories of Rig in the garage as he toned up cars.

Tey comes up to my side, throwing his arm over my shoulders while sniffing my neck with a groan. He doesn't care that I'm covered in blood and am a literal mess with mascara running down my cheeks after my eyes started watering as I sucked Nicky's cock.

I can't believe I did that. My mind is still reeling, and it's crazy to think how wet I got, as if I got off on showing everyone that Nicky is mine.

"How about you go shower, cherry? We'll meet you in the billiard room," Tey mumbles into my neck, taking another deep sniff of me, like I'm a drug he needs, before smacking my butt as he jogs into the house.

I can only shake my head, watching his tight ass in those black jeans until he disappears somewhere into the house. Why didn't he want to shower with me?

"Take your time, Tillie. Tonight was... a lot." Nicky takes the helmet from my hands, placing both helmets on a bench, and just towers over me as his eyes flicker back and forth, looking for something.

He looks worried. Is he worried about me?

"I'm okay," I promise him, placing my hand over his thudding heart.

I really am okay. I'm not scared little Tillie. I'm not going anywhere, I face my fears head-on now.

"See you soon, pet. The guys are going to be there for a while." Nicky steps back from me, his index finger trailing over the dove necklace for a second before he strides into the house.

I chew on my bottom lip, debating if I should follow one or both of them into the shower, but I glance down and notice my hands shaking. Is this adrenaline or everything from tonight catching up with me?

I walk into the house in a daze, somehow ending up in Dom's bathroom. I don't even remember turning on the shower. I tug at my clothes, needing them off suddenly, like

I'll die if I don't get it off my skin. Tearing at the leather, I step into the shower and sink back onto my heels, the hot water streaming over my body.

"Fuck," I choke out, wrapping my arms around myself as I shiver, not caring two shits if the water is scalding hot.

Being in that pit with so many predators, feeling their stares searing into my skin… Cruz's cold, blue eyes promised retaliation when I swallowed down Nicky's cock like I couldn't get enough. That part was true. I wanted to make Nicky tremble under my touch, even though I was the one on my knees, but I had to show Cruz that he doesn't own me. That was me telling him that he means nothing to me and I'm done being the Tillie that was afraid to even breathe in the same room as him. He'll never hurt me again.

Never again.

Repeating that over and over, I don't know how long I stay under the showerhead, but I eventually climb to my feet and wash the grime and icky feeling of phantom stares off every inch of my body. Feeling somewhat in control of my emotions, I get out of the shower and go through Dom's drawers until I find some clothing in my size. I don't know why seeing clothes for me in his room brings tears to my eyes, but it does. It's like him saying I'm here to stay, and this is your home with me. I select a purple, silk cami with matching shorts and walk barefoot out of his room once I'm dressed. I follow the low rumble of voices towards the billiard room and stop in the doorway.

Tey is leaning over the pool table, lining his shot up, and glances up at me with a wink just as he hits the white ball. His hair is wet, and strands of dark blond hang over his eyes, making me want to brush the pieces back. He's shirtless and wearing gray sweatpants—my weakness. All women's weaknesses really. It's basically telling you to stare at the sausage fest that's on display for all to see.

Shaking out of the lust that is clouding my thoughts, I look over at Nicky and have to grip the doorframe as my breath shudders out of me. His smooth, porcelain skin with hard muscles across his biceps makes me want to bite them hard until I leave an indent on his skin and I want to run my hands over his strong shoulders. His wet hair is down, and I have the sudden urge to run my fingers through the long strands. I think this is the first time I've seen Nicky with this much skin exposed, and I'm not complaining because holy fuck. He's got an eight-pack that has my fingers twitching to skim over the ridges, maybe lick them too. Definitely lick them.

I devour his tattoos with hungry eyes. The black dragon curls around his ribs and down the sharp edges of his side until it leads into his black slacks. My teeth sink into my bottom lip as I drag my gaze down to his belt, the clasp undone like he didn't bother to finish dressing.

"He's magnificent, isn't he, peaches?" Tey's voice is silky like velvet chocolate. It makes me shiver as he moves to stand behind Nicky.

I watch memorized as Tey presses his body against Nicky's back, his hand sneaking around the dragon and trailing down his abs oh so slowly, stopping just short of the edge of Nicky's belt buckle. My nails dig into the wooden frame of the door, holding myself back, but Tey taunts me with a knowing smirk as he gazes at me over Nicky's shoulder. I gasp as Nicky suddenly spins around, his hand knocking Tey's away and wrapping around his neck as he bends him backwards over the pool table. Nicky holds his grip tight, eyes burning hotly down at a smiling Tey.

"Come here, pet." Nicky beacons with his index finger,

taking his gaze away from Tey, but only for a second to make sure I'm following his order. My feet move across the hardwood floor before I can even think about what I'm doing. I'm not fighting it though. His voice calls to me with a dark promise that I want to listen to him. It will be worth all my pleasure. I stand at his side, my hip leaning against the pool table as I stare at Tey and the hand holding him down. "You do as I say and you get rewarded with pleasure, but you disobey and I will edge you over and over again until my name is the only word coming out of your mouth. Is that understood?" Nicky asks in that deep voice that lowers with each promise coming out of his sexy mouth, his fingers suddenly gripping my chin tightly so my gaze remains on him.

"Y–yes," I reply shakily, feeling my core clench with what's to come.

"God. I love it when you're in control. Gets me so fucking hard," Tey says cheekily, his breath hissing as Nicky glares down at him while he tightens his grip on the pressure points around Tey's throat.

"There's no God here. I'm your God. Say my name," Nicky threatens through gritted teeth, his breathing rough as desire makes every muscle on his body stiffen.

"No."

I'm not sure why that comes out of my mouth. Maybe it's the challenge, to see how far he'll go, or maybe I want to see his control snap? I'm a glutton for punishment, and if it's delivered by Nicky... I'll beg for it.

"You sure you want to go there, brat?" Nicky releases Tey, his attention now fully on me, which tells me I'm going to get very messy, even though I just showered.

Tey stands up gracefully from the pool table, standing

shoulder to shoulder with Nicky. It makes me feel small as their gazes burn bright with lust and hunger.

"I think she wants you to punish her, Nicholas," Tey declares, moving away to circle behind me, like a predator about to catch its prey. "Will you beg?" Tey whispers in my ear wickedly, his fingers winding into my hair at the base of my scalp before he tugs sharply. I whimper? Purr? Plead? I don't even know because my eyes roll into the back of my head at the sensation of both the pleasure and the pain.

"Beg us, brat, and I'll give you everything you've ever wanted." Nicky steps closer to me, his abs grazing my breasts while Tey tugs my hair until my back is arched.

I pant as I feel Tey's cock digging into my lower back, the piercing grazing against the bottom of my spine as he grinds against me with a growl. He honest to God growls. It causes my pussy to gush, that sound making my whole body shiver.

"Make me," I challenge back with a snarl as I grind my ass against Tey, a silent plea to fuck me already.

"Oh baby, you have no idea what you're in for now." Tey laughs, his sinful, pierced tongue drags across my neck in one long lick that makes my nipples harden into sharp points.

Nicky stares down at me silently, his plump lips slowly curling up at the corners until I know for sure that I'm in trouble. That smile is all Nicky; dangerous and really fucking hungry. All for me and our Tey.

I don't get any warning. One second I'm sandwiched between them and the next Nicky is twirling me around until my breasts are pressing into the padding of the pool table. He grabs my right hand and brings it over my head before I can react. Tey does the same to my other hand while I struggle, even though I'm hardly trying to escape. My breathing comes out fast, legs quivering so much that I feel like they might collapse any second now. I want this so bad. The sound of Nicky snapping his belt buckle through his pant loops makes me freeze.

What's he going to do?!

"Shh, Pet. This won't hurt, we'll make you feel real good. Trust us." Nicky pauses at my wrists, stroking his thumb back and forth over my pounding pulse.

I relax my body against the pool table, putting my trust in them to take care of me. My body wants to fight free from being restrained, but I know they won't hurt me. Leather slide along my wrists before looping around them until I'm truly trapped under their mercy, to do with as they please. I tug to test the belt holding me hostage at their mercy and find it to be tight but loose enough if I really want to escape.

"Fierce, little kitten. Only pleasure and pain for our girl," Tey says, running his hand up and down the back of my thighs until he skims the crease between my ass cheeks and thighs.

I only know it's his touch by the rings he wears, the warm metal making me shudder with each swipe of his fingers over my exposed skin. Oh so slowly, Tey drags his big hands up, squeezing my ass until he grips the waistband of my PJ bottoms. Biting my lip to try and keep my moans in, he slides my shorts down until they pool at my ankles.

Nicky leans over my back, moving the hair covering my face gently out of the way, and slowly slides his soft lips to the back of my nape.

"Are you going to be good for us, or does this sweet backside need to be warmed, turned bright red under my hand?" He bites my shoulder and threads his fingers under my hair, making the curve of my neck bend under his control as he tugs sharply.

Oh God. Bliss has my body shaking, pleasure and pain

making me spread my legs wider under his weight pressing on top of me.

At all once, his touch disappears and the warmth from his body is gone as he stands up.

A desperate whimper slips past my lips as I arch my lower back, needing one of them to touch me.

"Look at her. Displaying her delicious ass for us. Her pussy is weeping, it's drenched." A dark chuckle comes from the other side of my body, causing my thighs to clench, knowing he's gazing at my wet pussy lips.

"One touch and she's going to squirt all over the place. Maybe we should make her wait a little while longer. She's quite beautiful tied up this way." The finger that trails down my spine to the crack of my ass leaves me shaking uncontrollably.

He's right. I'm going to come so hard, soaking my thighs and the soft velvet of the pool table under me if he moves his finger a little higher.

I can't breathe, gasping into the crook of my elbow. I need to come like my life depends on it.

"Fuck you," I whisper, my voice heavy with need.

"There she is. Such a fucking brat. I'm going to smack the brattiness out of you, starting by turning this ass that's only ours fucking red with my palm. You'll feel me for days, toy." That's the only warning I get from the deep, lusty tone of Nicky's voice just as the palm of his hand smacks my right ass cheek.

Palm meets flesh, thudding with a sharp slap that echoes around the billiard's room along with my loud cry of pleasure. My ass burns, the blood pooling where the imprint of his palm smacked. I squirm as Tey's fingers trail around, sliding up the inside of my thighs. He finds me unbelievably wet, a gush of juices coats his fingers as he slips them back and forth over my sensitive pussy lips.

"Oh, she likes that. Do it again." Tey taunts me, delight and desire making his voice come out smooth but raspy.

The next slap makes me jump. Nicky's palm moves to my left butt cheek with three quick smacks before he gently rubs the burn with his big hands. My nails dig into the velvet red of the pool table as I stand up on my tippy-toes, my body preparing for the next spank. He doesn't hit me in the same spot, he switches to places I wouldn't expect. The back of my thighs, that sensitive, fleshy part at the bottom of my ass, his fingertips just barely grazing my pussy with each slap. Tears run down my face as I gasp for breath, needing them to touch me and put me out of my misery. Tey just keeps stroking any part of my exposed skin, the back of my neck with his pierced tongue, or rubbing his hands up and down my arms. I didn't even know those spots were sensitive.

"Had enough yet? Ready to beg?" Nicky asks, his voice slightly out of breath, excitement evident in his tone. I gulp, inhaling roughly as I push my hips out and up, silently begging him to let me find release. They both chuckle and step away from me, taking their body heat with them. "Tillie, Tillie." Nicky clucks his tongue and grasps my tied-up wrists, his other hand squeezing the meaty part of my hip, just as he quickly flips me over without breaking a sweat. "I want the next pretty words that come out of your mouth to be you asking us to fuck you, begging for us to fuck you hard. Until then, you're just going to get our hands on this beautiful body." Nicky slides his gaze down my body, taking in my scars, tattoos, and tear-streaked face with blazing, green eyes.

My cami top rides up at some point, stopping just under

my breasts, but Tey solves that problem by grabbing the hem and sliding it up until he pauses at my mouth.

"If it's not begging then I don't want to hear it." Tey taps my lips, telling me to open my mouth. "Good girl, and keep it there until you're ready to meet defeat." He winks as the material slips between my lips and I sink my teeth into it as I glare up at him.

He smirks, shaking his head as he sees that I'm not going to be begging. Tey leans down, his blond hair the only thing I can see as his lips wrap around my hard nipples and sucks. My gasp is trapped in the cloth, but my body begs for more as I arch into his mouth, and my eyes widen as I watch Nicky bend over until his mouth is inches from my other nipple. Warm breath makes me shiver just as he licks my nipple with small flicks of his tongue while Tey bites down on my other one. Pain shoots through me, but pleasure hits a second later, and has my toes curling. They slide down my writhing body, leaving a wet trail of kisses and licks. I practically shoot off the pool table when Nicky bites my hip bone and Tey leans over to lick that tender spot so slowly that my eyes roll into the back of my head. I open my eyes and glance down as they prop my feet on the edge of the pool table, my legs spread wide so both of them can fit between my thighs. All my focus is on them. The house could be on fire and I wouldn't even notice.

"Kiss me," Nicky growls with an order, gripping the back of Tey's neck in a firm hold to drag him closer.

Tey doesn't hold back, doesn't fight as he pushes his lips roughly against Nicky's. Their lips slide over each other, a power play of dominance. Two, deep groans echoes around me as their tongues stroke, Nicky quickly taking over the kiss. Sharp jawlines, muscles moving in their cheekbones as they keep switching angles, chests heaving as the kiss deepens.

Breaking apart, they stare at each other for a second and turn their gazes towards me. Eyes dilated, deepened pink lips parted, and dewy skin, all for my eyes alone.

"You like that, peaches? Don't worry, we won't leave you out," Tey coos and bends his head down, biting into the fatty part of my inner thigh.

I cry out, the sound muffled as I look down to see his teeth marks and a little bit of blood on my thigh when he draws back. Nicky drags his fingers up the inside of my thigh, sliding towards the entrance of my pussy, but keeps going as he collects some of my juices and smears it slowly around my clit like he has all the time in the world. Swipe after swipe, rubbing in small circles on my clit has my vision going hazy and my legs quivering. I'm already close. I'm about to come.

"I'm going to try something, but I need you to trust us one hundred percent, pet. Do you?" Nicky pauses, taking his gaze off my glistening pussy lips to look into my eyes.

I don't hesitate. I nod my head in confirmation, loving the shining approval in his gaze just as he slides two fingers into my pussy. He crosses his fingers, stroking my inner walls before sliding his digits in farther and curling them. He pauses, watching my breasts heave with each deep breath before he turns to Tey.

"Suck her clit. I'm getting her ready for both of us," Nicky orders, waiting for Tey to get to his knees between my wide, parted thighs. I watch Tey's head disappear between my legs and seconds later his hot breath has me grasping at anything to hold onto. The ledge of the pool table will have to do for now because Tey wraps those plump lips over my clit and sucks like his life depends on it. "Fuck. Yes, she loves that. She's cutting off the circulation of my fingers." Nicky hisses between his teeth, his fingers finally moving with small waves before he viciously rubs over my G-spot with a pleased, wicked chuckle at my reaction.

I scream behind the makeshift gag, my stomach tightening as I start to come when Tey flicks his tongue fast and hard over my clit. Nicky takes his fingers out as I squirt, shoving them back in and rubbing quickly before drawing back again. It feels like I'm never going to stop coming, my whole body shaking as I keep squirting. The pool table feels damp under my butt, my juices coating my thighs and Tey's naked chest.

"Holy fuck. I love when she does that," Tey rasps, breathing hard as he pulls away and looks up at me, but Nicky grabs his chin until he has no choice but to gaze up at him instead.

"How does she taste?" Nicky asks, shoving his fingers into Tey's mouth... The fingers that were just inside my pussy.

Tey wraps those wide lips around Nicky's digits with a groan, sucking off all my juices until his fingers are clean.

"So fucking good, but I think she can do better than that, don't you?" Tey questions Nicky, who turns back to me and, without warning, shoves three fingers into me this time.

My pussy quivers around his fingers, sensitive but fucking greedy as I clamp down on him tightly and try to grind against the palm of his hand as it grazes my clit with each thrust.

"Yeah, she can do better." Nicky's lip curls into a snarl, his eyes squeezing tightly closed with rapture on his face as he moves his fingers in and out of me while I gush around him uncontrollably. My moans are embarrassingly loud as he shoves his fingers deeper, curling them until he's stroking my G-spot, hitting that spot over and over until I'm trembling. All I can hear around me is the pool table balls clinking together in the pockets, my panting breaths, and the blood rushing in my ears. Just before I'm about to come again, he pulls his fingers out and steps away. I cry out in dismay behind the gag, wriggling in the restraints with tears of frustration leaking down my cheeks. "Tey. Get up and get on the chaise lounge with her on your lap, facing me," Nicky demands, trailing his fingers, shiny with my cum, across his bottom lip and groans as he tastes me.

Chest heaving, Tey stands up from between my open thighs with wet lips and swoops me up with an arm behind my back and the other under my knees without breaking a sweat. I take the gag out, welcoming any punishment for disobeying Nicky's orders, and lean forward to bite hard on Tey's pec so he's carrying my mark too.

"Pudding... Do that again." Tey grins down at me in his arms with longing and huffs as he lays back in the lounge chair, arranging me on his lap with ease until I'm facing Nicky.

My heart races, feeling like it's going to jump right out of my chest and crawl its way over to Nicky. I hope he shows mercy and handles my bleeding heart with love because I'm not sure I can take any more heartache.

I lean back on Tey and loop my restrained wrists around his neck while spreading my legs wide on either side of his strong thighs. This is me giving my trust away.

Exposed and vulnerable.

"Tillie... you're fucking beautiful spread out like this. All ours, to do with as we please. Look at this wet pussy. I can't wait to feel you squeeze both of our cocks." Nicky straddles the end of the lounge and rubs my legs as he stares down with hunger in his eyes at my holes all open for him.

Tey shudders behind me, his chin resting on my shoulder as we both watch Nicky's hands slide farther up my legs until he's pushing the inside of my thighs. He spreads me so wide that my muscles are straining and shaking, but it's worth it as he leans down and his whole freaking mouth covers my pussy. The top of his mouth grazes my clit, and his bottom lip is right at the entrance of my cunt. His long tongue moves up and down in slow sweeps, slurping my juices with moans leaving his mouth. Each wet squelch is loud and crude, but I don't give a fuck.

"Jesus, Tillie. We are going to fuck this pussy until you're hoarse in the throat and crying." Tey's warning is deliciously dark while his hand snakes around my waist and strokes my pelvic bone as he moves lower until he's inches away from Nicky's mouth.

He runs his hand through Nicky's hair almost lovingly, and that distracts Nicky enough that he pauses and looks up with hooded, almond-shaped eyes, red cheekbones, and glossy, panting lips covered in my arousal. Tey glides his thumb over Nicky's wet lips and covers my clit, rubbing in small circles that makes me jerk.

"Keep eating her out, Nicholas. Get her ready for us," Tey urges, his cock grinding into my ass as his thumb moves faster and faster.

Nicky groans deeply in his throat and immediately puts his mouth back on my pussy... devouring me like a man starved.

"Please. Oh God. Yes! Right there. Don't stop!" I rasp out, begging shamelessly around a moan, my hips moving so I can grind against Nicky's sinful mouth.

"Give her more. She's about to come," Tey says in excitement, his breath fanning against my neck as he watches over my shoulder, never once pausing as he viciously rubs my clit without mercy.

My body shakes as I grip Tey's hair at his neck while my stomach tightens and my moans turn into screams of pleasure. Nicky backs off at the last second again, just as I was about to come. Three, thick fingers slide inside my pussy, stuffing me full as he slides his fingers in and out rapidly. It sets me off without warning.

We all watch as I squirt around his fingers the moment he pulls his hand away, soaking his abs and Tey's thighs under mine. I can hardly breathe, my chest heaves and my legs spasm with each slide of Tey's fingers stroking slowly over my clit. They don't give me a break, it's almost painful, but it feels so good that I never want it to stop.

"That's it, pet. Give us more," Nicky encourages, his sinful smile dark as he slides four fingers inside of me.

I suck in a gasp, back arching as my inner walls grip him hard. Too full. Too many sensations at once. I'm so wet that his fingers slide out easily, and plunge back in with a squelch.

"Ever been fisted, cherry?" Tey whispers, licking the shell of my ear before biting down hard enough to sting.

"N–no. Fuck," I manage to choke out, my body strung tight as Tey puts all of his fingers over my clit and rubs back and forth so fast that I'm about to come again.

I watch, as if in a daze, as Nicky pulls his fingers out and makes a tight fist, his hand resting at the entrance of my pussy as he looks up at me with a smirk.

"Oh, pet. I do love taking your firsts. Scream for us." The deep lure of Nicky's voice leaves me feeling delirious and high on endorphins.

I hold my breath as he starts to push his fist inside my pussy, my lower lips spreading wide around the intrusion as his hand inches slowly into me. My head tips back against Tey's chest as the pressure becomes too much, my pussy fluttering around his fist.

"That's it, baby. Just a little more and his whole fist will be in. Look at how beautifully you suck him in. Such a greedy little cunt," Tey breathes out in awe, his fingers stalling over my clit, making me cry out at the loss of the orgasm that was building rapidly inside of me.

"Oh God." I suck in a gasp, my head snapping down and staring in disbelief at Nicky as his whole fist comes to a stop with only his wrist showing.

"Not God, pet. Say our names," Nicky demands darkly, his fingers flexing inside of me like a pulse as he oh so slowly slides his fist out until my pussy is gaping around his knuckles before he shoves it back in hard.

"Nicholas!" I cry out, my eyes watering from the intense pressure that hurts but feels good at the same time, as he starts fucking me with his fist in a steady rhythm that makes me want more.

Tey bites my neck, his pierced tongue running up the length of my vein that is pounding uncontrollably. He laughs against my skin, biting down as he suddenly slaps my clit with the tips of his fingers. My whole body jerks, my inner walls clamping down on Nicky's fist as he fucks me faster and faster.

"Say. My. Name," Tey orders with every slap, his fingers hitting the same spot each time, and he doesn't seem like he plans on stopping anytime soon as my body withers on his lap.

"Tey." My voice comes out shaky and needy, my toes curling from the pleasure building in my core.

My inner walls contract around Nicky's pumping fist as the most powerful orgasm slides through my whole body. I think I black out for a second, my screams sound distant but loud at the same time.

"Good girl. Fuck, that's hot." Tey growls like an animal, his fingers gently circling my clit as I calm down from the highest feeling of pleasure.

I blink rapidly and glance down as Nicky pulls his fist out, his hand making a wet suction sound. More of my cum squirts out of me, creating a puddle underneath us.

"Now you're ready, pet," Nicky states in a calm tone, but it almost sounds like there's a threat lying underneath his words.

I shake, a full body shudder, and I'm not sure I can take anymore. I absentmindedly play with Tey's hair on the back of his neck, wondering if this is what other people feel when everything inside yourself feels complete. Every little piece in your life starts to make sense, the good and the bad. It was all leading to this moment when everything just clicked into place.

"What are you thinking about, peaches?" Tey hums in my ear as we both watch Nicky stand up and take off his pants without looking away from us.

"I love you both." I grin wickedly as Nicky narrows his emerald gaze at me and quickly takes off his underwear, his cock slapping against his abs.

It's hard to keep my gaze off his tattooed cock, wanting to take in every detail, but I want him to know that I'm serious. I really do love him. I'm not sure if he's even heard those words before, but I plan on giving all my love to him, to them, every day until I die.

"I. Love. You. Nicholas." I state each word slowly, letting him absorb what I'm saying as his eyes close before popping open with a burning desire in their depths.

"Now you did it. I love you too, Nicholas," Tey says,

chuckling as Nicky clenches his teeth, taking me by surprise as he lunges forward.

He doesn't waste any time as he grabs Tey's pants and tugs them down to his ankles in quick movements, his hands shaking as if he can't contain what he's feeling.

Probably scared and happy, I'm not going to pressure him, but I see how he looks at me. I know he loves me and Tey.

My ass shifts over Tey as I lift to help his pants come off easier, and it doesn't shock me that when I settle back down on him, he's commando. The air rushes out of me as I glance down to where Nicky is sitting right between our spread thighs, his masculine hand grasping Tey's hard cock. Up and down he strokes, his thumb grazing Tey's piercing with each slide.

"Oh, shit. Fuck." Tey hisses in bliss, his hands reaching around me to grab Nicky's face and he pulls him in close until I'm sandwiched between them.

I hold my breath, not daring to blink so I don't miss anything as Tey roughly slams his lips onto Nicky's. It's like watching two violent ocean waves crashing into each other, fighting for dominance, and neither is giving up until it turns to calm waters.

Tey flicks his tongue along Nicky's bottom lip before tugging it into his mouth to suck. My fucking nipples tingle as I watch them. Everything is slow and seductive. Masculine and passionate.

Nicky breaks away with a deep groan and turns his head, capturing my lips in a kiss that is surprisingly gentle but hard, as if he's holding himself back.

"Take us, Nicky," I beg, biting his bottom lip hard enough to draw blood. He rips away from me, his bloody lips in a snarl, but I can see the pained and scared look in his eyes. "Please," I whisper, not breaking eye contact as he guides Tey's cock towards my pussy and rubs the mushroom-shaped head through my slippery lower lips.

"I must be dead. This is heaven, isn't it?" Tey mutters behind me in a dreamy but strained voice.

"Not heaven. Hell. This is hell, Tey. Tillie tortures us every day with her beauty and her sweet as fuck pussy," Nicky says in a serious tone, leaving me breathless.

I fell such a long time ago, I'm not even sure if heaven would take me now. But, I'll take hell if it means I can love and be loved.

My head tilts back onto the muscular shoulder behind me as Nicky guides the tip of Tey's cock inside of me and pauses as he sits up on his knees. He scoots closer between my spread legs and fists his pulsing, unbelievably hard cock. I stop breathing as he slides his tattooed cock alongside Tey's before he starts to push his cock inside of me too. The feeling of two cocks inside one tight place is painful, but the ecstasy is too good to describe, as Tey helps him by placing his hands on either side of my pussy. He spreads me open, his breath ragged in my ear as Nicky slides inside with a wet suction. I would feel embarrassed by the noises but I'm too far gone. This is taboo and dirty and I love every fucking second of it.

"So fucking tight, Tillie," Nicky rasps out, sweat sliding down his chest as he inches forward, moving his cock right alongside Tey's.

I can only moan, holding still as Tey lifts his hips under me to pump his cock with small jerks until my inner muscles start to relax around them.

"Fuck."

"So tight."

"Ah!"

I'm not sure who's cursing, or if I'm screaming. All I can feel is deliciously stuffed to the max. They bottom out at the same time and stop so my body can adjust, but I just want them to move. It's too much. I wiggle in between their bodies, loving their agonized groans of pleasure as I move. Nicky starts to pull out, Tey doing the same before they slide right back in with one long, smooth glide. At this point, I'm pulling Tey's hair so hard but he just thrusts his cock into me harder.

"Please, fuck me. Harder," I plead, needing them not to treat me like I'm breakable.

"You want more?" Nicky pants, leaning forward with his left hand supporting him by gripping the back of the chaise lounge behind my shoulder.

"Yes, yes, yes," I chant as Tey grips my waist with both hands, his nails digging in hard enough to draw blood as he jackhammers himself into me from below.

Nicky's abs flex as he rolls his hips, taking his time fucking me and ignoring my frustrated whimpers.

"You beg so prettily. Say please," Nicky says in a deep voice that causes my pussy to clench around them.

"Please," I whisper shakily, my legs already quivering.

Tey slows down as my pussy flutters around them, my orgasm right there. He glides his hands down my sides, the callouses making me shiver, and I have to wonder what it would feel like if he was cutting off my air. Would the rough pads of his palms hurt? I want that. I need it like I need my next breath.

Tey slides his hands around my thighs, gripping the insides and hooking my legs over his inner elbows until I'm laying back on his stomach with my ass in the air. I'm so completely spread open that they probably know my body better than I do.

"Say it louder," Nicky grunts out before sliding in until he can't go any farther. I can feel him bump Tey's cock as they both slide out together before slamming back inside.

"Please. Hurt me!" I shout, turning my head to the side so they can't see the shame in my eyes at my confession, that I need pain mixed in with my pleasure.

"I knew you were made for us the moment I saw you," Tey pronounces through each hard thrust, fucking me faster and faster while digging his fingers so deep into the thick part of my thighs that I know I'll have bruises.

I finally turn my gaze back to Nicky when he doesn't say anything, his pace never changing, and burning, green eyes swallow me whole. There's so much desire and need in that one single look.

"Say it again," he grits through his teeth.

"Hurt me," I plead, this time without looking away, seeing the flash of admiration in his gaze.

"Don't worry, pet. I'll hurt you so good, you'll be screaming around our cocks and begging for more," Nicky warns before he draws almost all the way out of me as I glance down.

His cock is shiny with my juices, making the colors of his tattoo stand out more so it almost looks like the dragon is going to devour me. He slams into me, slides out just as fast, and does it again and again. In and out, his control starts to slip away as he fucks me hard and rough. Tey keeps up with him, his groans deep in my ear as he glances over my shoulder to see my breasts bouncing with every hard thrust.

"This fucking pussy, milking our cocks. Our slut," Tey claims and clamps his teeth onto my neck, breaking skin until I feel the wet drops of blood trailing down to my breasts and navel.

Nicky watches with hungry eyes. I'm pretty sure Dom's

chair is destroyed as I hear a ripping sound over my head where Nicky is gripping the back of the lounge. With his other hand, he squeezes my breast before letting go and making me yelp when he slaps my nipple.

Back and forth, he switches until my nipples burn and are a bright red. He flicks his gaze up from my breasts and must see the tension on my face.

"More?" he asks, but he already knows the answer.

I nod, my breathing erratic. My eyes dilate as he wraps his fingers around my throat, a light hold, as if testing me until it tightens with each hard thrust.

"Fuck. Choke her, Nicholas. I'm going to come. Your cock feels so good sliding against mine, all slippery and hard in this tight pussy." Tey's voice becomes gravelly, his cock pumping into me so fast that my inner muscles clench and flutter.

I'm about to come. I feel every nerve ending from the roots of my hair to the tips of my toes. I can't catch my breath as Nicky cuts off my air supply, his face blurry as white dots dance in my vision.

"Come for us. Right fucking now!" Nicky growls, thrusting so hard and fast that the lounge chair scrapes against the flooring, moving with each slap of his hips against my ass.

My legs tremble in Tey's hold, my stomach clenching, and my hearing is only narrowed down to the sound of our bodies slapping together.

"Ah! Yes! Yes, yes, yes! Please, don't stop!" I scream out, my pussy convulsing around their cocks and squeezing tighter the harder they rut into me.

I can't stop, it feels like it's never going to end. Each time they slide their cocks back out, I squirt, making a mess all over us. Ecstasy flows throughout my body, leaving me feeling high and dizzy.

"Shit. Fuck. I'm coming." Tey grunts, his hips jerking, and a second later, with a roar, he fills me up with jet after jet of thick cum.

Nicky groans deeply, but his cock never stops thrusting, even as cum spills out of me. His whole body is tight, muscles straining, and his eyes are wild. He's holding back.

"Let go," I grit out, grinding up against him as his body shakes.

His head tilts back, resting on his broad shoulders as he starts to come, his face contorted in bliss. His neck muscles and veins pulse as his cum coats my inner walls, spurt after spurt. He stops himself from collapsing onto Tey and I by gripping the chair over our heads once more, his breathing rough near my ear. We don't move, the only sound in the room is our panting breaths.

"I must be dead. I'm not even mad about it," Tey wonders out loud. He sounds delirious and happy.

I laugh and let out a groan as my pussy flutters around their cocks. Nicky lightly kisses my lips with his soft but swollen mouth before he pulls back, his gaze down as he watches his cock slide out of me. Tey lets go of my legs and lifts me, his cock slipping free and slapping against his abs. I can't help but watch the cum gush out of me. Our cum. It's a lot. Nicky slides his fingers through it and pushes most of the cum slowly back inside of me, making me moan at the pinch of pain and pleasure.

"I like this, seeing your messy pussy covered in our cum," Nicky says as he stares at his fingers pumping in and out of me, his tone possessive and hard.

"Hell yeah. Is it baby-making time?" Tey asks excitedly

and I wiggle, trying to sit up but Tey grabs my hips to hold me still.

"I'm kidding, sweetcheeks. I haven't canceled your doctor's appointment for the birth control shot. Don't worry. I got this. Let's go use that big-ass tub in Dom's room and snack on cheese with some wine!" Tey rambles, sitting up quickly with me in his arms. He hands me over to Nicky in excitement before dashing out of the room, buck ass naked.

"What... What just happened?" I ask in amusement and a hint of fear.

He really wouldn't mess with my birth control, would he? Who the hell am I kidding? He is not making any future doctor appointments for me or coming with me. Christ. If he had his way, I bet there would be a bunch of babies crawling around here that look just like Tey.

"Let's get you cleaned up, pet. You did so good." Nicky avoids my question, leaning down to kiss my temple and I can feel his lips moving against my skin.

I love you.

Dalton

"This shit is fucked up, Prez," Axel comments from beside me on his bike, the faint glow of his cigar is the only thing to be seen in the alleyway.

I grunt, agreeing with him as I watch federal agents surround the area a block over at a crappy apartment complex. Dom brought a moving van to the warehouse, and we loaded up the scared women and children in there while making sure our faces were covered with the skeleton masks. It makes me sick to my stomach seeing their dirty, hollow faces. At least these people have a chance now, a new life they can make for themselves.

"I'm heading out. Going to meet Logan. Watch and make sure it all goes smoothly," I order, clapping Axel on his back as I rev my bike and pull out onto the street.

The wind whips in my face and the bike vibrating beneath my calloused hands calms my thoughts for the brief moment I have before I arrive at my destination. Downtown Chinatown. Tonight was a clusterfuck. Every single time... every goddamn time I witness Jin's sex trafficking ring, I feel more and more helpless. I've known Nicky for a long time now, and I've seen what his father's business does to him. It eats you alive from the inside, rotting and festering until not much is left. I'm sure if Nicky didn't have us growing up, I wouldn't even recognize who he'd be to this day. Probably just like Jin.

There was a while there, I feared he was turning out like the stone-cold monster his father is. I think my little bitch brought back that spark of hope with her strength and the ability to move forward in life, no matter what is thrown her way. She's it for me, and I'll be damned if someone tries to take her from us. I'll strike a match and watch everything burn without remorse just to have her at my side.

Seeing her tonight on that fucked up display stage filled me with so much rage. I was seconds away from snapping necks and leaving a trail of bodies in my wake. The only thing that stopped me was the power she held over everyone, no one could look away. They were captivated as she knelt at Nicky's feet, but in reality, she was standing taller than anyone else in that pit. Seductive, with a lure you can't help but want to touch to make sure she's real. I know she can handle anything, even when her body shakes with vulnerability or the fear that grips her tight. In the end, she's always going to come out standing, and that right there is power. Something Jin or Franco will never have.

I know why she ran onto that stage and protected that little girl. It's in her blood to keep fighting, but now Jin has his sights on her even more. She ruined his business tonight and made him look weak, and that's not going to go over well. We need to bring them down faster before it's too fucking late.

That cocksucker is a coward. My old man used to say the same thing. He hides behind his business and lets everyone else do his dirty work. The Feds won't get anything from the women and children about who kidnapped them. Jin never showed his face. Even tonight, he was the voice of the show but stayed in the shadows. The moment gunshots went off, he disappeared and left his son to handle the rest. Little does Jin know, Nicky has been tipping off the Feds for years, telling them whenever someone was sold.

Being a hacker comes with its perks. You can hack into anything without ever showing your face, and spill secrets that most people wish they could take to the grave. Jin's days are numbered, and I can't wait to see Nicky take over the triad, his father watching as his son gains power just before his death.

I stick to the backstreets, going the speed limit because wearing a Hell's Devils vest is a beacon, and the last thing I need is to be pulled over by a cop who isn't on Franco's payroll.

Before long, I'm pulling into the crowded streets of downtown Chinatown. I figured it would be deserted, but no. People stroll by, the smell of food permeating the air and bright lights giving the illusion it's not one in the morning.

I pull up to the curb outside another one of Jin's buildings. This is where most of the drugs ship out from, and his office is above the restaurant that he owns. Shutting off my bike, I run my hand over my hair with a sigh. Showtime.

Striding into the restaurant, everyone turns to look at me with suspicion as they eat their meals. Most are the Triad taking up space to watch who's coming through the door, but if you live in this neighborhood, you know to look the other way if you aren't working for Jin. I don't bother looking at anyone, instead, I walk into the kitchen like I own the place and ignore the hateful looks thrown my way. Yeah, they don't like bikers and it's very obvious.

Pushing through the swinging doors, I take the stairs two at a time and roll my eyes as I reach the top. Jin's minions line the hallways leading to his office and a few guards reach for their guns when they spot me. I smirk, knowing they aren't going to do shit. I'm tempted to sucker punch one of them and see how many I can fight off or kill. I'm not picky.

Logan stands by the door at the end of the hallway and looks at me with a blank face. He can't fool me. His left eye always twitches when he's pissed off. I hope it's a murderous twitch because I could do some more killing tonight. We didn't kill enough of the bidders tonight, too many got away from the gunfire.

Shame.

"Lo." I cross my arms and raise a brow while glancing at the closed door of Jin's office.

"He and Franco are having a little chat," Logan grinds out, his eye starting to tick some more.

"Yeah. Fuck that. I don't take orders from anyone," I state with a snarl and shove past him, throwing open the office door without giving a shit if I'm interrupting their little powwow.

I'm the fucking president of the Hell's Devils. Nothing and no one tells me what to do.

Fuck them.

My gaze connects with Jin first. The smug fuck is nice and safe behind his desk as he counts money into piles. The only way you can tell he's mad is the small tick in his cheek, otherwise, he looks like it's just another day in the office.

The office smells of some sort of incense and the aroma of food from the restaurant underneath. It's also hot as hell in here. There's only one running fan by the window, but I think Jin just likes to make people sweat. It makes you uncomfortable and nervous as your stomach sinks with that sick feeling.

"Where's my son?" Jin asks in a cold, dead voice and

reaches for another stacked pile of money to flick through as he counts.

Logan comes to stand beside me, his hands clasped behind his back, but I would bet my motorcycle he's palming his gun that's always in his belt at his lower back. We both stand there, not saying anything, covered in fucking soot from the fire. I hope my dirty boots leave stains on his flooring.

"Busy. He's on-site at the warehouse to make sure everything runs smoothly," I reply gruffly, staring him down with my arms folded over my chest.

I'm not scared of him, and he's going to learn one day that he's just a man who will be staring down a barrel.

"Is that so? I just got off the phone with Franco and he was asking where you all are." Jin slaps his hand on the hard surface of his desk in anger and grabs the TV remote, turning up the volume.

I look at the screen and grit my teeth when I see Franco on the news giving a statement, acting like the concerned Chief of Police.

"As of right now, we don't know how the fire started or how many casualties. We are looking at the scene and will know more soon. There's been raves around these parts, so we are hoping just a few kids were messing around. I care about this city and its safety. We will find answers, and in the coming days, the drugs on the streets will be seized."

Franco's voice drones on and on about bullshit, answering every question the reporter has with an easy smile. He's charming, saying the right words, but he's a lying bastard. The people of Los Angeles don't know this, they see someone who can clean up their city. He's going to make it to governor, it's a gut feeling I have. We'll have to move plans up faster before that ever happens.

"How about you start again and move out of my guest's way? You're blocking the door." Jin gestures behind Logan and I as he hits mute on the TV again.

My shoulders tense. I don't like knowing someone is standing behind me without them making a damn sound to alert me. Moving away from the doorway, my nostrils flare as Cruz steps into the office with purpose. I look out of the corner of my eye at Logan, his pupils are dilated and eyes narrowed on his target with death in his gaze. Shooting my hand out, I clamp it on Logan's shoulder and squeeze so tight that I'm pretty sure I'm crushing his bones.

"Not here, brother. It's not your kill. Remember that." I whisper so low that only he can hear me.

Logan shrugs my hand off and straightens his suit jacket before clasping his hands behind his back again, but I can hear his teeth grinding.

"He's busy. Did your clients make it out?" Logan asks, changing the subject to something that's going to have Jin blowing a gasket.

I can't take my eyes off of Cruz, watching as he plops himself down on the couch under the window and lifts his feet up onto the coffee table. He meets my gaze with a smirk, like he knows something I don't.

If you look past the dead, blue eyes of his, you can see the murderer's rage underneath the surface. I refuse to break eye contact first, letting him know who's the fucking alpha in the room.

"My clients are either dead or never doing business with me again," Jin states calmly, and that raises my hackles. "But luckily, Cruz can help with that situation. He's agreed to supply me with new, shiny merchandise that anyone in the market looking for fresh meat won't be able to resist."

Motherfucker!

"When you see my son, and he's done playing with his pet, I want to see him. I want that fucker, Dom, dead, his head on a spike! I know it was his gang that interrupted my auction. I'm putting a price on his head," Jin demands harshly and snaps his fingers just before he gets back to counting money.

Barely-clad women enter the room with silver trays of cocaine, offering some to Lo and I, but I just glare until they walk away in their high heels. One of them bends down to Cruz and cries out in pain as he grabs her wrist, dragging her down until she's sprawled out on his lap. He grabs a baggie of pure powder and dips his pinky in, holding it to the girl's mouth until she opens up. He rubs the cocaine along her gums and draws a straight line on the top of her breasts before snorting it.

"Tell Tillie I'll be seeing her soon. I have to take a road trip but I'll be back before you know it," Cruz says, not even bothering to look our way as he watches the girl on his lap sway from the drugs before pulling out a knife from his pocket.

It takes everything in me to not launch across the space separating us and snap his neck. Logan walks stiffly out of the office without saying another word to Jin because we were clearly dismissed. I see the first glimpse of blood and a swipe of the knife on her skin with the curve of the letter C.

"Leave," Jin states darkly, and I feel like my boots are full of lead as I walk out of the office without a backwards glance.

I follow Logan, not saying anything as we walk down the stairs and back through the front of the restaurant until we're outside. His stride is stiff and angry as he walks to his car that's parked in front of my bike.

"Lo," I say and watch him take a deep inhale before looking over his shoulder at me. "We'll get them."

He nods and hops into his car, speeding away with tires screeching. I didn't ask where he's going because I already know. I follow on my bike through the city and into the rich neighborhood until we're pulling into Dom's driveway through the guarded gates. I feel like if I don't see Tillie's face right now, I'm going to go crazy and start hitting anything within my reach.

I shut my bike off, swing my leg over it and jog through the doorway Logan has left wide open for me. I don't hear anything at first until I walk farther into the house, heading towards the kitchen where men's voices are talking in a low tone.

Standing in the doorway, I choke on my spit and hold back a laugh as Tey talks to Dom, buck naked. Tey's naked in Dom's kitchen, holding a bottle of wine and a package of cubed cheese.

"My cupcake deserves the best of the best. She needs pampering, amigo. Don't throw a fit. I'm heading to your master bathroom to give our girl the most amazing bubble bath she's ever had," Tey declares cheerfully while pulling the already-open wine bottle cork out with his teeth, spitting it at my feet with a grin and taking a swig.

"Jesus. I love my queen and know she deserves it all, but don't make this a thing. My fucking eyes burn." Dom gestures to Tey's naked backside and strides towards him to grab the wine bottle while heading out of the room.

"Bro... it's like you have a death wish. Cover your junk, man. Did Lo come through here?" I ask worriedly, sounding like an old, cranky grandma, but I saw the look in Logan's eyes tonight.

He's fucking mad and a bit unhinged, and I'm worried

he's going to go guns blazing without telling anyone. He's gonna get himself killed.

"Told him Tillie is naked and in Dom's bathroom." Tey shrugs and tears the cheese package open as he strolls out of the kitchen.

Everyone is losing their damn minds around here, and I'm the only one who is san—wait. Did he say my little bitch is naked? I turn on my heel and run to catch up with Tey just as he rounds a corner and walks into Dom's bedroom like he owns it. I hear Logan and Dom arguing before I even see them. I roll my eyes as I step into the bathroom that smells of lavender and vanilla, not the least surprised that these two are bickering like clucking hens. It's a bromance in the making and entertaining as hell.

"I don't give a fuck if you're surrounded by an army at your disposal. Jin just put a price on you. Anyone and everyone will be gunning for you now. Fuck!" Logan shouts, pulling at his hair until it sticks up at every angle.

"Don't worry about me, little Russo. You're about to see how the big boys play. I can handle myself and keep everyone safe in this house," Dom says calmly, cursing in Spanish as he yanks at his cufflinks in frustration before collecting himself.

Scary fucker. I shiver. It's always the ones that are in control, on a tight leash, that break first. God help anyone in their path. I've been waiting years to see Logan break. That day will go in the books.

"Lo." Tillie's voice is soft and sweet, coming from the mountain of bubbles hiding her naked body from me in the tub. "Get in so I can hold you."

That's all she has to say for Logan to growl like an angry bear as he throws off his jacket, but struggles to loosen his tie and grows impatient with his buttons. Tillie is leaning against Nicky's shoulder on one side, and on the other side is Tey with a goofy grin on his face as he cuddles into Nicky's neck. Nicky is just sitting there with his arms crossed over his chest with a blank expression, like he's some badass, but his lips keep twitching as Tey feeds Tillie cubes of cheese.

Logan finally groans and barrels into the tub with his button-down shirt and pants still on. He sits on Tillie's other side and drags her into his arms, looking like he doesn't plan on letting go anytime soon. He's going to need her for the moment, I think, given the worried look Nicky and Tey are throwing at him.

I glance at Dom and shrug before stripping down to my black boxer briefs and getting into the water, sitting across from our girl. I grab her foot and start massaging the arch with the pad on my fingertips. Moments later, Dom climbs in naked as well with the wine bottle. He tips it back and swallows a gulp before passing it around to Tey.

Who in the fuck has a tub this huge? Did he foresee a future where he would need one this big to fit a tiny woman and a group of big dudes?

"So, bubble bath group time is a thing, I'm taking it?" Dom says slowly, staring at Tillie with a fond expression on his face as she scoops up bubbles and blows them in his direction with puckered lips.

"Oh yeah. With five of you and my poor vagina, I'm going to need to rest the girl as much as possible. I'm sore as hell. They wrecked my pussy," Tillie comments as she runs her hands through Logan's hair while staring at Nicky and Tey with a sated grin.

"Damn it! I missed the double dipping," I groan out miserably, tilting my head back against the tub's ledge.

"Don't worry, big guy, you can take her ass next time," Tey coos and coughs as Tillie splashes him with a gasp.

"Absolutely not! Sorry, baby, but that monster dick of yours isn't coming anywhere near my ass," Tillie admonishes, her dark eyes sparkling with mirth at my horrified expression.

"We'll see." I narrow my eyes at her in challenge as I tip my head towards her, drinking in her tan, smooth skin that has a soft blush from the steam of the water.

"Logan, you ready to hear what we found?" Nicky breaks the easy, light mood, and I know it has to be discussed but damn.

"Just tell me," Logan mutters into the crook of Tillie's neck, as if he wants to bury himself under her skin.

"We found a file in Jin's office. I'm sorry, brother, but it was never Dom's father who killed your mom. Jin already knew about Franco sniffing around his drug business. There were photos of you and your... mom in the file. He had the triad following Franco, learning everything about him, including his weaknesses." Nicky pauses, clearing his throat like he's unsure if he should tell him the rest.

"He killed her, didn't he?" Logan rasps out, his body shuddering as he squeezes Tillie closer.

"I'm sorry." Nicky takes a deep breath. "Jin framed Dom's father and killed her himself instead."

No one says anything after that. Logan's whole body is stiff, except for the small shake in his shoulders. I hate seeing my brother in pain. Tillie whispers quietly in his ear, stroking his hair until he finally lifts his head with red eyes pinning us all on the spot.

"He dies." That's all he says as he takes turns looking us each in the eyes as we nod until he lands on Dom.

"They will all pay for their sins by our hands," Dom

promises, passing the wine bottle to Logan, as if a peace offering.

Logan reaches over and chugs until the bottle is almost empty before placing it on the tub ledge and cuddling back into Tillie. She looks worried as she stares at him before gazing over at Dom.

"Thank you for getting those women and children out of there tonight," she warmly replies, leaning over to stroke her palm down Dom's cheek.

"Always," he simply promises, as if he'd do anything for her.

"They're safe with the Feds," I announce, reassuring her, rubbing my hand up and down her calves as silence settles over us

"We need a fun day. It's decided! Tomorrow we forget all this shit and pretend that hell isn't raining down on us. I know the perfect thing. I did promise you a dance, didn't I, pudding?" Tey breaks the thick tension in the air and glares at anyone who dares argue with him.

Well, it seems bubble baths with a bunch of naked dudes is in my future, and whatever fucked up shit Tey's planning for tomorrow.

I can hardly wait.

Tillie

"Baby girl, I don't think now is a good time to go out. What if something happens to you?!" Logan thunders in sexy Italian under his breath as he paces back and forth in Dalton's club bar while Hell's Devils watch him warily.

I don't blame them. Logan looks like he's had better days. His hair is a mess, the usually perfect strands are disheveled, as if he's been running his hands through it constantly. Seeing his iron-pressed, white button-down untucked from his pants and the top few buttons undone makes me feel bad about what I'm going to do today to him, but it's necessary. I need to trust him, and it's the only way for me to see if he's with me the whole way.

"This is why it's the perfect time to go out. We can't do this day and night, Lo. This isn't living, and I'll be damned if I'm stuck in a cage again. Either you're coming or we leave without you." I fold my arms across my chest, shifting in Dalton's lap as he adjusts me until my ass presses down over his hard cock.

I don't know how they do it, walking around with strain-ing, rock-hard cocks most of the time. Does it hurt whenever they have to tuck it into the waistband of their pants? Doesn't it get uncomfortable having that thing pressing down their thighs like a third leg? I shudder at those thoughts, thanking Jesus for granting me with a vagina. Small miracles, I guess.

"Calm the hell down, bro. You need this. We need the break... You need a break," Dalton says in a gravelly voice with no room to argue. "Besides, the Hell's Devils and Dom's gang will be watching the area for any threats. This is happening."

"Fuck me," Logan groans and starts to reach for the whiskey in front of me before I quickly swipe it away, throwing back the whole drink without a grimace.

Fuck, that burns! What the hell is this stuff? Dragon's fire? My chest is on fire.

"No. You aren't drinking anymore. You went through two bottles of wine last night and you look like shit. Consider this our date, Lo." I don't hold back, giving Logan shit just as he does to me.

"You're trying to kill me, aren't you? Okay, baby girl. I'm going to go shower and get presentable for our date. You know, the one I didn't even get to ask you on," Logan grumbles and scowls at the floor, but a faint smirk tugs at his lips.

"Stop being a big baby. You get grumpy when you're not relaxed, and if you're a good boy, I'll make it worth your while later tonight," I purr seductively, tipping Logan's chin up with my index finger until he's looking me in the eyes.

Dalton nearly spits his drink out just as he was taking a swallow of beer. He whispers *holy fuck* under his breath at our display, watching with rapt attention. Usually, Logan is the one throwing the shots, being bossy as hell and demanding, but seeing his body relax under my touch and his eyes darkening with lust, it would seem he wants to let go of that control that he holds so close.

Guilt is eating me up alive, and I hate the feeling. I wish I could just hold him again like last night, being safe in his arms, letting him know it's going to be okay, but I can't. Tonight is going to be the beginning of us or the end. I won't lie, I'm a tad excited to play with him though.

"I'll hold you to that," Logan says, leaning across the table and kissing my lips delicately. I'm wondering if he knows how fragile we are right now.

One small mistake and it will shatter us. After tonight, I plan on making sure that nothing can ever come between us again. He's about to meet psycho Tillie.

Logan pulls back and stands with a stretch, groaning before he walks away towards the back of the club and Dalton's room.

"Are you going to tell me what you're planning? Don't try to lie, I felt your body tense up as he kissed you." Dalton rubs my leg over my jeans and his other hand spreads out across my waist, his thumb gliding back and forth over the exposed skin between my pants and shirt. "I know you don't trust easily, and I don't blame you. Sometimes I wonder how we got so lucky to have you because we sure as shit don't deserve you. What I'm trying to say is, I'll stand back and let you do what you have to, but just be careful. For both of your sakes."

Dalton shocks me into silence, the low grumble of his tone warming my heart as he kisses my temple and lifts me off his lap. He sets me back in his seat and is about to step away but I grab his wrist. He looks over his shoulder with a raised brow, a question on his face.

"Thank you. That means a lot to me, baby." My throat grows tight and it takes everything in me not to cry. "You deserve every piece of me. It takes a real man to know his wrongs."

"Fuck, little bitch. You are killing us." Dalton's expression is pained as he spins back around and crouches in front of me, grabbing my chin between his fingers.

His lips move softly against mine before deepening the kiss, gliding over my mouth with a passion that lights my body on fire. It's hard and almost shy of desperate, as if he can't get enough of me. I know the feeling. It's like this every time I'm around my guys. He sucks my bottom lip into his mouth and nips just as he pulls away with a serious expression.

"I'm going to need you later. Not right now because I have a feeling you're going to need your strength tonight, and you probably don't want to be walking funny." Dalton chuckles at my heated expression before standing and walking away while whistling—the cocky fucker.

I giggle, actually giggle like a schoolgirl, and take a deep breath as I close my eyes. Life is funny, you literally never know where it's going to lead you... Mine has taken me for a wild ride with some real bullshit but it's not so bad now. I mean, it can still be shitty some days, like yesterday at the auction. At least I wasn't alone, and afterwards, it just proved that I'm never going to be alone again. I have five sexy as hell, protective men that love me.

Like I said, life isn't so bad.

"What has you smiling like that, sugar plum?" Tey startles me as he whispers in my ear and makes grabby hands when my wide eyes meet his.

"Jesus Christ! Tey! Don't sneak up on me like that." I laugh as he continues making grabby hands as he bends down and throws me over his shoulder.

My hair swings in front of my face, blocking my view as

he walks out of the bar area and down a hallway until he stops at a closed door. Plus, I get to watch his tight ass in black jeans while just hanging around.

"We have two presents for you, sweets," Tey says excitedly, smacking my butt and squeezing before bending to set me down.

The room spins for a second, and I'm pretty sure my face is red as I grip Tey's forearms to steady myself.

"We?" I ask, staring into his gorgeous, bright blue eyes.

"Pet." Nicky presses against my back, his soft but deep voice making me shiver. "Here, let us help you put this dress on."

I lean my head back onto his shoulder, loving the feel of his minty, hot breath on my neck as I close my eyes. I don't bother questioning what dress or what they're planning, because I'm deliriously happy at the moment. This must be what love drunk means.

"Lift," Tey whispers, as if he feels this too, the calming and easy way we just fit together.

He taps my wrists and I raise them over my head while he grabs the hem of my tank top, slowly dragging it up my body until I hear the fabric dropping onto the floor. I smile when I hear Tey's low inhale and the pleasing hum he lets out under his breath as he takes me in. I didn't bother wearing a bra today, just my jeans and pink tank top. I feel Nicky's rough hands grip my hips, kneading his fingers into my flesh before sliding towards my jeans. He unsnaps the button and drags the zipper down with a slowness that is killing me, desire burning low in my stomach like a struck match. I shimmy my hips as he drags my jeans down, tugging them over my ass with a hard yank.

"This ass," Nicky praises, growling as he grabs each ass cheek, kneading the thickness of them in a bruising grip.

"One day I'm going to fuck these tits and coat you in my cum." Tey flicks his tongue piercing over my hard nipple, circling it in wet laps until he bites down with a tug.

"Please," I whimper, moaning wantonly in my throat from the sensations and the deep ache in my still sore pussy from last night.

"Oh, how I love it when you beg, but I love it more when you're needy and desperate," Nicky's voice is downright dangerous, like setting my panties on fire dangerous, while he steps away from me and takes his body heat with him.

My eyes pop open in disbelief as Tey moves away too, but at least he's pouting like I am.

"Get back here and make me come," I order, glaring over my shoulder as my body is wound tightly with horniness and need.

"Here, pretty lady, lift your arms." Tey snickers, reaching behind me to grab something off the bed, and quickly shifts the silky material over my arms just as I obey, lifting them over my head without really thinking about it.

The dress glides over my body, barely feeling like I have anything over my skin. The feeling makes me shiver and as I glance down, I notice my nipples standing out like two beacons that say look at me against the red silk. My God. It's breathtaking and fits me like a glove, molding to my shape perfectly.

"Exquisite and all ours," Nicky breathes out against my neck, brushing his lips there for a second until he produces something in front of my eyes.

He holds up a syringe, filled with some type of liquid and flips it between his fingers as I narrow my eyes with suspicion.

"You aren't drugging me again," I calmly say, trying not to cross my arms over the silk material, so it doesn't wrinkle.

"Not for you, pet, but don't worry. If you want to be fucked while unconscious, I always have more where this came from," Nicky says in a deep, throaty voice that has me gulping loudly and sweating bullets.

Would I like that? Jesus. I don't even know, but I've done things I never thought I would like, so I think maybe I would.

Looking between the two of them and eyeing the syringe, I definitely like the idea of them using my body for their pleasure.

"Oh God. I'm so fucked," I mutter to myself, shaking my head to clear my thoughts before taking the syringe from his offering hand. "What is it and what's it for then?"

"It's to knock Logan out. He'll be conscious one second, and out like a light the next. It's just a little tranquilizer," Tey giggles like a schoolgirl with his eyes sparkling like he's staring at precious gems or his unicorn.

"Okaaay. I'll just put it—" I furrow my brow, thinking about where I can hide this thing, but I just shrug as I stuff it between the girls. Tey and Nicky smirk, eyeing my boobs that are squished together in this dress, high and perky. "Chop, chop, boys." I clap my hands and twirl to find a pair of black heels on the bed. "Let's do this. The wicked rest for no one, and I'm feeling very wicked tonight."

I giggle at their heated looks as I bend down to slip on the heels and practically sprint out of the room as Nicky growls and Tey makes grabby hands again. Anything with violence and danger turns them on... It doesn't help that I have breasts either.

"Get back here, brat! I changed my mind! I'm thinking your ass needs a spanking!" Nicky shouts after me, and I can hear both of their thudding steps behind me as I run as fast as I can in high heels.

"Suckers," I whisper to myself, smirking because that was my plan all along, but he can spank me later.

I'm on a mission to test Logan's love for me. I pray he doesn't fail, and I don't break.

I never want a man to break me again, and that thought alone steels my spine, more determined to go through with this, even if it breaks my heart.

"You want another drink, Mama?" Dom strokes my bare shoulder, making me shiver at the simplest touch.

Music pounds in sync with my heart while the soothing sound of the ocean plays in the background. The moon is high in the starry night sky, and bodies grind together on the dance floor with the seductive beat of the music as liquid courage flows through them. Since we arrived at the bar on the beach, something inside of me just settled. It's not crazy busy, almost relaxing with the low murmurs of voices, and the twinkling lights the bar has strung up makes it look like you're closer to the stars. I love it. I haven't danced yet because we headed straight to the outdoor couches near a gas fire pit the moment we spotted them right off the dance floor. My body keeps swaying to the beat of the music as I cuddle into Dom's side, the heat he's giving off helps with the slight breeze from the ocean.

"Yes. God. These margaritas are strong. I'm pretty sure it's just tequila, but it's so yummy." I hum in delight and sip up the last of my drink until I'm only sucking up air.

"Your cheeks are looking a little pink, cupcake." Tey chuckles as I lower the empty glass and stick my tongue out at him.

Of course he takes that as an invitation and leans

forward from his seat next to me, his pierced tongue swiping up from my chin to cheek. Laughing, I wipe my cheek and quickly grab his chin before he can pull away. His blue eyes, that holds me captive every single time, shows so much love for me.

"I licked it so it's mine." My voice comes out raspy, practically a purr as I slowly dart out my tongue and lick his cheek as I turn his head to the side.

He groans deep in his throat and turns his face towards me when I let go of him and lean back into Dom's embrace once again.

"I'm all yours, peaches. You can lick any part of me you want." Tey winks, adjusting his cock in his pants, right in front of my face, before he turns around, heading right towards the tiki bar with a sexy swagger.

I watch his tight ass walk away in those black jeans that cling to all his muscles and look to my left to see Nicky watching him with a heated gaze too.

"I'm going to make sure he doesn't get into trouble or stab anyone," Nicky says as he clears his throat, standing from his chair and striding towards the bar with a sexy swagger.

More like stalks towards the bar, Tey in his sights, just waiting to be devoured. I shiver in pleasure, my thighs clenching, and I'm praying to fucking God that Nicky takes charge again. I would be most willing to sit back and watch the show, seeing all the delicious muscles on display as he ties up Tey.

"Cold?" Dom mutters with a cocky chuckle near my ear, his hand rubbing back and forth on my thigh where the dress has inched up, exposing my skin.

"No." I bite my lip and notice Dalton staring across at

me, his eyes dipping down to trail over my body before meeting my gaze.

"You look cold, little bitch, but don't worry, daddy can warm you right up." He pats his lap, spreading his legs wider as he leans back in his seat while looking over the edge of his beer bottle as he takes a drink.

Dom sighs and brings my hand up to his mouth, kissing my knuckles before releasing me. I smile up at him, my fingers trailing over his short, black beard as I lean up to kiss him on his chin.

"It's going to take a while getting used to having to share your attention, but it's all worth it to see you happy, Mama," Dom says huskily, his eyes stalking me as I stand up and smooth my dress down.

"You'll always have me, papi." I wink, adding an extra sway in my hips for him as I round the fire pit and come to a stop between Dalton's spread legs.

I glance over to my right, looking at Logan as he swirls his whiskey in his glass while tilting his head back to look up at the moon. My stomach dips like a roller coaster, taking in his disheveled appearance and the five o'clock shadow he usually keeps clean. I ache for him, and everything he's feeling right now, I'm right there with him. I have to remind myself that what I'm doing is for the best. It's only going to make us stronger, if he makes the right choice. It takes everything inside me not to walk over to him, cuddle into his chest, and tell him that it's going to be okay. His pain is my pain, but until we settle the block between us, I'm going to have to keep my feelings locked down tight.

It's for the best.

I keep repeating that as I glance back at Dalton to see him already staring up at me under his lashes, his violet eyes bright in the reflection of the fire. I need a minute to breathe, to hold strong, because even now, my body is leaning towards Logan, and I'm seconds away from calling tonight off and just forgiving him.

"Dance with me," I choke out, desperate for a distraction.

Dalton tilts his head, looking back and forth between my gaze before he gives a single nod. My body sags in relief as he stands up, towering over me, and grabs my hand in his much bigger one.

"Always." He doesn't waste a second and spins me around right as we get to the dance floor so my back is to his front, swaying back and forth to the slow yet sexy beat of the music. "Relax. We have you, you're safe. Dom's guys are watching all the shadows move, and the club is right over there, on high alert in case something happens." Dalton points to his club members, all of them in leather vests hanging around the bar and seats while being alert as they drink.

"I'm trying. I won't let anything happen to you guys also," I vow hotly, knowing if it came down to it, I'd do whatever it takes to prevent my guys from being killed.

I feel the tension drain from my body as Dalton wraps his big arms around my waist, his hands spanning my whole stomach. Placing my palms over his, I give him a squeeze and drop my head back onto his collarbone. His body moves so easily with mine and he's graceful and light on his feet for a big guy.

"That's it, little bitch. You feel so damn good in my arms." His voice gets all gravelly and low, sending tingles down my spine as he drags me impossibly closer to his body until we're squeezed tight from head to toe.

One song leads into another and everything just melts away. This is what I've always missed. It's not about putting on a show or dancing seductively to capture someone's attention. This is just me dancing with the man I love, protected and safe.

"Can I cut in?" Dom's smooth, sexy voice appears in front of me and I didn't even know I had closed my eyes until that point.

Dalton grumbles, almost reluctant to release me, but he swings me out, Dom catching me as I gasp at the unexpected move. The song turns into something more upbeat, sultry, and sexy. Latin music. Dom smirks down at me, his dark brown eyes warm as he starts to move us. His hand slides down my spine until it's resting just above my ass while his other grips the back of my neck so I'm forced to only look at him.

It's fucking hot, the way he controls our movements with confidence. He moves sensually and fast, yet he just flows with the music. I can't help but laugh as he spins me out and back in while moving his hips to the beat. Each time he spins me out or swings me under his arm, he always places his right hand back on my neck.

"Beautiful." He pulls me closer as the song slows to an end and places a kiss on my forehead while I draw in a deep breath of his scent.

Always smokey, like a cigar but sweet. Cherry and spice. It's addicting.

"Baby cakes! You look so good dancing, I couldn't look away from your sweet, peachy ass. Here's your margarita, although I did take a few sips. Now, step back and I'll show you how it's really done on the dance floor." Tey hands me an almost empty glass with a wink as he talks really fast while making shooing motions with his hands, as if he needs the whole dance floor to himself.

"Might want to step back. It's like nothing you've ever

seen before," Nicky says as he comes to stand by our side, his arms crossed over his chest, smiling while watching Tey nod to the DJ.

My jaw drops.

"I–I have no words..." I choke out, trying not to laugh as Tey starts to jump around when the music starts.

I'm not even sure I'd call it dancing. He kind of reminds me of a jelly bean bouncing around or a dolphin jumping out of the water, but he doesn't care, and his smile is so big as he places his hands together behind his head and rotates his hips. I can't hold it in anymore. I burst out giggling, shaking my head as he winks again at the sound before he flips onto the ground and starts to do the worm.

"It's only going to get worse. Nicola called," Nicky states quietly, not taking his gaze off Tey. "She said she picked up the package and the room is all set." I bite my lip, sinking further into Dom's embrace for courage and I look around for Logan. He's not in the same spot I last saw him, the glass he was holding sitting on the side table empty. "He's on the beach." Nicky looks down at me, his face serious, but he gently moves my hair behind my ear as he gives me one single nod.

That's all I needed. Exhaling, I glance over my shoulder to Dom to see him already staring down at me.

"You can do this. Whatever you need, mama. I'll help you along the way," Dom mutters so matter-of-factly that I straighten my spine and pull out of his arms, knowing he's right.

I can do this.

"Come get us in ten minutes." My hands shake as I walk away from the dance floor, passing Dalton who tips his beer at me and winks.

These fucking men. They have so much faith in me that

it makes me feel like I can take on the world. Just one to go to determine if we'll make it or break it.

I slip my heels off as I get to the sand and scan for Logan. He's not hard to find, and my heart breaks just looking at him. He's sitting on the sand, his shirt unbuttoned and whipping behind him as the wind picks up from the ocean. Goose bumps pebble my arms as I take quiet steps towards him. Seeing his shoulders hunched as I sit down right next to him and the faraway look in his eyes as he stares out into the water almost makes me back out of the plan. I have to remember this is for the best. It's going to heal us both.

"You should be back up there with the guys. I'm not the best company right now, baby girl." Logan's voice is raspy and low as he continues to stare out at the water with his face expressionless.

He doesn't fool me, though. He's telling himself he wants to be alone so he can bear all his pain by himself, but it will eventually eat him up inside the longer he holds in all that misery.

"I'll stay right here." It's the only thing I say as I lean my head on his shoulder and just stare at the ocean too. He doesn't say anything for a while, but at least he's not telling me to leave. "Lo?" I whisper as I rest my chin on his bicep to look up at his face and place my hand that's holding the syringe behind him on the sand.

"Yeah, baby girl?" He looks down at me, his light brown eyes so sad and hurting that I want to cry.

"You remember the last time we were at the beach and you said how you'll always protect me?" My voice shakes as I bite my lip to hold back the tears, hating the sharp pain in my chest with what I'm about to do.

So much pain between us and mistrust.

Never again.

He doesn't break my stare, his gaze flicking back and forth between mine like he's looking for something.

"Yes, I'll do anything to protect you," he quietly says, his voice so hushed with emotion, a million expressions crossing his face.

Regret, guilt, and the one that catches my attention most... love for me that's so strong my breath gets taken away. This man owns me.

"You didn't protect me from one thing though. It hurt so bad that I can still feel it." I uncap the syringe with two fingers as I sit up on my knees with my hand still behind his lower back, turning my body towards him because I'm going to look him in the eyes with my next words.

"Who hurt you?" His eyes grow dark, his tone turning menacing and threatening.

Raising my hand up behind him, the syringe hovering on the other side of his neck, I take a deep breath and plunge the needle into his skin right between his neck and shoulder.

"You did," I whisper, feeling tears trailing down my cheeks as I see his confused expression and the instant pain flashing in his hazy eyes as the drug takes effect.

Within seconds he's slumping forward and I catch him in my arms, moving his hair out of his eyes to stare down at his peaceful looking face.

"Don't let me down, Logan." I place a kiss on his soft lips and pray he doesn't break my heart.

CHAPTER 16

Logan

"Wake up." A deep, muffled voice that strangely sounds like Darth Vader has me blinking my eyes open with a painful groan. Whoever woke me up is looking to die today.

Everything is blurry as my chin is tipped down towards my chest and I have a killer headache pounding like I have the worst hangover. With slow movements, I lift my head and blink rapidly to clear my foggy vision. I'm staring at a blank slab wall in confusion with two metal chairs directly in front of me, the lighting so dim that it takes me a second to get my bearings at what the actual hell is going on. My body jolts the moment it becomes clear where I am.

Did someone really fucking kidnap me?

"Good. You're awake, it's time to play."

My head whips to the side, taking in the shadowed figure by a metal door. They're hiding their voice behind a voice box that sounds like he or she is about to tell me they're my father. I wouldn't put it past Franco to put me in a torture chamber just for shits and giggles, but hiding in the dark isn't his style. So who is that sticking towards the shadows?

"You made a big mistake, asshole. I'm going to enjoy ripping you to shreds," I grind out, feeling the cold metal biting into my wrists as I lean forward in this fucking uncomfortable chair.

I'm not surprised I'm chained in cuffs, but it does come to my advantage that the long chains are bolted to the floor and gives me enough room to lift my arms up to shoulder height. If they come close enough, I can wrap my arms around them and squeeze until their bones are being crushed in my hold.

"I–I wouldn't do that if I were you. You don't want your girl to die, do you?" the voice asks, clearing their throat before delivering that threat.

My veins turn to ice. They have Tillie?

"I'm going to murder you! Slice and dice you open until your guts spill out!" I roar, my muscles straining as I struggle to break free until I'm breathing hard like an animal with wild eyes.

"Bring them in!" Darth Vader shouts, backing towards the door until he or she is plastered against it. "You only get to choose one, the other dies."

With that, he slips through the open door into a dark hall, and a second later, Tillie stumbles into the room in her underwear and high heels as someone pushes her from behind. She isn't wearing a bra, her breasts are completely exposed, and I can feel my pulse pounding in my neck knowing these assholes are looking at her naked.

A man, judging by his height and build, dressed all in black with a ski mask, lays his hands on her to shove her again. He's another addition to my kill list. Another girl is pushed in as well, but I can't take my eyes off of Tillie, looking to see if she's injured. Both of them are directed with shoves towards the metal chairs right in front of me and tied down with their hands behind them.

"Lo–Logan?" Tillie's voice shakes as the blindfold over her eyes is whipped off by one of masked men and her big, brown eyes connect with mine.

I can breathe easier seeing she's not injured, and I need her to know I'll protect her always.

"Baby girl, it's going to be okay. I'm not going to let anything happen to you," I growl out, promising her with everything in my body that she won't be hurt.

Her eyes soften slightly as she looks me over, taking in my naked form except for the black brief boxers they left me in.

"I believ—" she starts to say, but a shrill, shrieking voice next to her has that soft look in her eyes disappearing with a blank expression.

My brows wrinkle at that look as Tillie turns her head to the side and I barely glance at the other woman who keeps struggling in her chair. Just as the last man leaves the room, the door is slammed shut and everything goes quiet... until it doesn't

"Logan! Oh my God! Baby, are you okay? Where are we?!"

My eyes widen and I look quickly over to the right in shock as I stare right at a terrified, disheveled Paris.

You only get to choose one, the other dies.

Well, that is starting to make sense now.

I shout over and over, making sure that whoever is listening knows my answer.

"Paris!"

EPILOGUE

Rig

"Rig, you have a visitor! How nice! I'll let you two chat, he's more active today," the bubbly nurse says in a cheery voice. She doesn't see the panic in my eyes as she talks behind me to the only visitor I ever get.

I can't move my body or speak, but my eyes work. I stare down at the dirty biker boots as he walks around to kneel at the side of my wheelchair.

"More active, huh? Would you mind sending in the doctor? I have a few questions." Cruz stares at me with empty, cold eyes, but he smiles charmingly at the nurse who gushes over him before she walks out of the room quickly, muttering under her breath.

I can't move or speak. All I'm good for is listening and watching. It's been this way for years, ever since Cruz got the drop on me and admitted me to Ridgeway Psychiatric Hospital in Oregon.

Whatever the doctor pumps into my veins leaves me feeling crippled and barely here most days. It's the same routine every day. Meds, sitting in this god-awful wheel-chair, staring out the window at the pine trees, shit, eat, bathe, and repeat. My body is a vegetable, wasting away each day until I'm going to be nothing, as long as those fucking pills are shoved down my throat. I'm a strong man, a biker at heart. I can take whatever life throws at me. Being stuck with my own thoughts, having someone else wipe my ass... it's torture, but I can live through it.

What I can't live through are these visits from Cruz. I hated the kid the first time I saw him, the fake mask he puts on for everyone didn't fool me. I should have watched him closer. I should have dug a hole and buried him in it. I was too late because now I have to listen to him describe in detail, every single time, exactly what he did to my Tillie.

This is a torture no father should have to go through. I failed my little girl, and I'm reminded of that each time he visits.

"You know, old man. When I put you in here, I had my doubts at first. Just kill the old biker and be done with it, I told myself, but then I got to thinking... Where's the fun in that? I thought I'd just leave you miserable for the rest of your sad excuse of a life. Telling you over and over how I raped your niece's sweet ass, passed her to club members like she's just another hole to be filled. Last time I was here, I almost considered ending your life. Just a little bit too much morphine and off you go, but imagine my surprise when I learned that Payne wasn't dearest daddy." Cruz stares into my eyes, flickering back and forth as he waits for my reaction.

He doesn't have to wait long.

My eyes widen in panic as my dry mouth tries to open in a scream of anguish, but only a gurgled groan comes out before my cracked lips.

"Oh, this is what I was missing the whole time. To see the fear in your gaze, exposing your weakness." Cruz breathes in deeply, his eyes closing in bliss as he leans in closer until he's looking at me again with a gaze void of any emotion. "It's almost like I can taste your panic, your pain. These must be feelings."

Cruz chuckles, looking unhinged as he closes the gap between us and kisses my forehead as a tear leaks down my cheek.

"I'm going to enjoy watching the world crumble around you, seeing all hope fade from your eyes as I take Tillie all for myself. Remember this, Rig." Cruz stands, gripping my shoulder as he walks around my wheelchair to whisper in my ear. "She's not your daughter, niece, friend, or anything else. She's mine. All mine."

I slowly blink, clearing my blurry vision as a figure steps through the open doorway out of the corner of my eye. I want to be able to move, even if it's just my hand so I can wrap it around Cruz's neck and keep squeezing until the life drains from him and into my waiting hands.

"Ah, Doc. Glad to see you're still keeping your patients calm and happy. I have a certain package for you, pure crystals." Cruz dangles a white powder baggie from his fingers as the doctor steps into my view. He quickly grabs the coke and puts it in his white jacket.

"Have some respect, this is my workplace!" the doctor hisses between his teeth, looking over his shoulder at the doorway, and upon seeing it's empty, his shoulders relax.

"Easy doc. No one knows you're an addict for cocaine. Your secrets are safe with me, as long as you keep Rig here on drugs to keep him nice and paralyzed." Cruz claps the doctor on the shoulder, enjoying as the little man shrinks into himself at the way Cruz is towering over him menacingly.

"O—of course. Whatever you need," the doctor stutters,

gulping loudly as he glances quickly down at me and then back at Cruz.

"I'm so glad to hear that because I'm going to need a few months' supply to keep him this way. He's coming with me to see his daughter."

I hear Cruz's words echoing as if he's far away, his gaze hitting the back of my head with such evil intent that it practically burns into my skin.

I scream in my head, staring straight ahead at the swaying pine trees and being able to do nothing in the frozen, weak state I'm always in.

Not my little girl. Anything but her.

TO BE CONTINUED

Up next...

Psycho Punks (dolls and douchebags part five)

Last book

AUTHOR NOTE

I knooowwwww! I said this would be the last book, but I couldn't help myself. All the characters wouldn't shut up, so we are getting a fifth book.

Sooooo... How are we doing?! Everyone okay? Take a deep breath and don't throw your kindle or come at me with a deep hatred for that cliffy. I can't wait to hear about your reactions to this book and any theories that will all be uncovered in part five. I love all my readers and hope you enjoyed this book even though I'm leaving you guys hanging until the next book. The final freaking book in this series. It's been a wild ride. Thank you so much for reading, sharing, and reviewing.

STALKING LINKS FOR MADELINE FAY

Facebook Group: https://www.facebook.com/groups/270252770540820/

Newsletter: https://www.subscribepage.com/MadelineFayNL

Facebook like page: https://www.facebook.com/madelinefayauthor/

Instagram: http://Instagram.com/Madelinefay_author/

TikTok: www.tiktok.com/@madelinefayauthor

Hive: MadelineFay

www.madelinefayauthor.com

ABOUT MADELINE FAY

Madeline lives in rural Michigan in a castle with all her fur babies and husband. She loves to read, you'll find her in her tower with her kindle and drinking Boba tea. She has a few addictions, chocolate is her weakness and anything seventies related. She's a hippy at heart. She likes to pretend she's a main character in a Korean drama and listens to Kpop, mainly BTS. She has an evil day job, but at night she watches over her city in the shadows and calls herself Batman. Not really but she keeps hoping it might come true one day. She's in her bat cave writing and plotting mad, evil genius stories while sipping some wine.

www.ingramcontent.com/pod-product-compliance
Lightning Source LLC
Chambersburg PA
CBHW031454160726
47994CB00005B/2028